MW01105238

# THE TOWER ROOM

# THE TOWER ROOM
## ELLEN HOWARD

A JEAN KARL BOOK

Atheneum 1993 *New York*

Maxwell Macmillan Canada *Toronto*

Maxwell Macmillan International

*New York   Oxford   Singapore   Sydney*

Atheneum
Macmillan Publishing Company
866 Third Avenue
New York, NY 10022

Maxwell Macmillan Canada, Inc.
1200 Eglinton Avenue East
Suite 200
Don Mills, Ontario M3C 3N1

Macmillan Publishing Company is part of the Maxwell Communication Group of Companies.

First edition

Printed in the United States of America

10 9 8 7 6 5 4 3 2 1

Library of Congress Cataloging-in-Publication Data
Howard, Ellen.
The tower room / Ellen Howard. —1st ed.
p.   cm.
"A Jean Karl book."
Summary: When she goes to live with her aunt in a small Michigan town, Mary Brooke discovers a secret room that becomes her refuge as she tries to cope with all the changes in her life brought about by her mother's death.
ISBN 0-689-31856-1
[1. Mothers and daughters—Fiction. 2. Aunts—Fiction. 3. Death—Fiction.] I. Title.
PZ7.H83274To   1993
[Fic]—dc20                                        92-39240

# TABLE OF CONTENTS

# CHAPTER 1

# THE CASTLE

It looked like a castle!

Mary Brooke peered through the taxi window at the house and felt a ripple of excitement. Yes, it *was* this castle-house they were stopping in front of. In front of which we are stopping, she corrected herself. Mary Brooke was determined not only to speak properly but even to think properly. One's diction, Miss Osgood said, was a measure of one's quality.

"At last," Aunt Olive was sighing. She clutched her thin black handbag on her lap while she waited for the taxi driver to open her door.

Mary Brooke slid across the seat after her and climbed from the taxi.

"Is *this* where you live?" she asked, breathless.

"Of course it is," said Aunt Olive. She was fumbling in her handbag for the key. "You know that, Mary Brooke.

You visited us several times before your grandmother passed away."

While Aunt Olive went to open the door, Mary Brooke stood on the icy sidewalk and gazed up at the house. She had been told of those visits before, but she couldn't remember them. It had been years ago, and—I'd think I'd remember it was a castle, she thought.

Of course, it wasn't *really* a castle—only a large house built in the middle of a small, slightly sloping lawn. On either side were quite ordinary houses, the sort of solid brick houses people lived in in small towns like this one. That was partly what made Aunt Olive's house surprising. You didn't expect to find anything so—*fanciful,* Mary Brooke thought, the word rising in her mind like a bubble—in a town like Kirkland.

The house was built in two short rectangular wings, and between them, nestled in the angle where they met, rose a turret with an arched doorway at its base, a tall arched window near its top, and a weathercock on its conical roof.

It's a tower for a princess, thought Mary Brooke, and immediately the thought came: Oh, I wonder if *my* room will be in the tower?

"Aunt Olive, Aunt Olive!" Mary Brooke cried, running up the slippery walk. She jostled the driver, who was struggling with their suitcases, and he shot her a surly look.

"Watch where yer goin'!"

"Mary Brooke, *please!*" said Aunt Olive. "Just set them here in the entry," she said to the man.

"But, Aunt Ol—"

"Mary Brooke, I said *please!*"

Mary Brooke stopped at the bottom of the steps and

sulked down at the flagstone beneath her feet. Aunt Olive was paying the driver, counting the money carefully into his hand and then adding a quarter tip.

"Thank you, ma'am," he said, tugging at the brim of his cap.

He gave Mary Brooke another unpleasant look as he brushed past her, but she paid him no attention. She was gazing upward again, up at the narrow tower window with its diamond-shaped panes. What was behind that window? she wondered. What wonderful sort of room— what sort of *chamber*, Mary Brooke corrected—awaited her there?

"Come in, come in!" Aunt Olive was saying crossly. "Don't just stand there when the door is open, letting in the cold. It will take long enough as it is to get the chill off the house after being away so long. Do come *in*, Mary Brooke!"

Mary Brooke took a deep breath, climbed the three steps to the little stone porch, and walked into the castle.

She stood just inside the entry hall, which was the bottom floor of the turret, and looked about her as Aunt Olive removed her gloves, pulling at the tip of each finger, one at a time, as Mother used to do, until the glove was loosened and slid off easily. Aunt Olive was sighing. She seemed to sigh a lot, Mary Brooke had noticed, and her sighs meant different things at different times. Right now they meant she was glad to be home, Mary Brooke guessed, and gazing at the plastered walls of the turret, hung with dim pictures in heavy gilt frames, suddenly Mary Brooke was glad too. Not glad to be home, for this was not *her* home, but glad to be somewhere she could stay for a while. She was tired of being shuffled about, she thought, and somehow it seemed fitting that she should wait here. A castle was where a princess should wait for rescue.

"Aunt Olive," Mary Brooke said, "shall my room be in this tower?"

Aunt Olive gave her a startled look.

"Of course not, child. There's only a tiny unheated room up there—a fancy of my father's, your grandfather's. Mother had it blocked off after he passed away. I've had the blue room made up for you. It was Isa—your mother's when she was a girl. Actually, it's the prettiest room in the house. Take off your coat and hat and hang them here in the closet. Your galoshes can go there, and your mittens. Then I'll take you up."

The staircase rose from the entry hall, on either side of which Mary Brooke caught glimpses of a cavernous living room and dining room. She looked for the blocked-off door to the tower, but saw nothing.

*The room that had been her mother's . . .*

Mary Brooke steeled herself as she thought the words. She felt quite calm, she told herself. It did not hurt to think of Mother. Of course she would miss her, but she was used to missing her. Even before Mother's illness, Mary Brooke had often gone days at a time without seeing her.

"I can't just sit home!" Mother used to say. Mary Brooke could see in her mind how she used to look, sitting at her vanity table—wherever they moved, Mother took her vanity table—with all the little bottles and jars set out before her on the vanity tray. She would be gazing into the mirror at her own beautiful face as she painted the scarlet outline of her lips, while Mary Brooke hung behind her, careful not to bump her elbow. "I'm still *young*," Mother used to cry. "I deserve some fun, don't I, Brooksie? Doesn't Mommy deserve to have some fun?"

When Aunt Olive opened the door to the right of the top of the stairs and carried in the large suitcase—Mary Brooke had managed the small one by herself—Mary Brooke recognized instantly that this was indeed Mother's room. Of course, it was much neater than Mother had ever kept a room, but the blue satin spread on the white-and-gilt bed was exactly what Mother would have chosen, and the vanity with its frilly skirt and mirror was prettier even than the one they had lugged from place to place. Another long oval mirror between two windows reflected back to Mary Brooke the image of her own pale self. The room was large and many-windowed and chilly. On a sunny day it would be a sunny room, Mary Brooke thought, but now it made her feel small and exposed.

Aunt Olive was lifting—again with much sighing—the heavy suitcase onto the vanity bench, which she had pushed against the wall.

"I'll help you unpack," she said with another sigh, and this time Mary Brooke thought the sigh meant that she, Mary Brooke, was a great deal of trouble.

"I can do it myself," Mary Brooke said rudely, though she had not meant to be rude.

"Very well," said Aunt Olive. She glanced at the small gold watch on her wrist. "There isn't much in the house to eat, but I expect we should have a bite of something fairly soon. I'll call when it's ready."

She paused at the door and looked back at Mary Brooke. "After supper I'll show you the rest of the house, so you'll know where things are. And we'll talk about the rules."

As soon as Mary Brooke heard the stairs creak beneath Aunt Olive's feet, she went to the windows to draw the drapes. They were long satin drapes of the same powder blue as the bedspread. There were windows on three walls, and as she pulled the long drapery cords, one after another, shutting out the wintry light, the room grew dim. Mary Brooke looked about for a light switch and found one by the door. She switched it on, but the high, cold ceiling light wasn't what she wanted either, and she switched it off again. She went to the table by the bed and pulled the little chain on a low blue-shaded china lamp. That was better, though its bluish cast made the room seem chilly. It was not a good reading lamp, Mary Brooke thought, but Mother had never read. Mary Brooke imagined she got her own love of books from her father, though Mother had never said so, only said sometimes in that whining tone Mary Brooke found irritating, "Brooksie, *must* you have your nose forever in a book? Talk to me, sweetie. Put the book down, there's Mommy's little love."

There were tiny light bulbs around the vanity mirror. Mary Brooke found the switch and turned them on too. That seemed to help shrink and warm the room a little. She looked about her and found herself sighing—like Aunt Olive, she thought with a small laugh at herself. When Father comes to take me away, I shall have a room of my own, fixed just the way *I* want it, she thought.

This room was almost perfectly square, but in one corner the wall bulged inward in a curve. Mary Brooke walked to it and cocked her head to one side, considering. It was the wall of the tower room, she thought. Just on the other side of that wall was the "tiny unheated room" Aunt Olive had spoken of—of which Aunt Olive had spoken. Grandfather's fancy, she had called it. Mary Brooke searched the smooth plaster for signs of a blocked-off door but found nothing.

Finally she turned away to her suitcase and began to

6

unpack the clothes, which were folded on top of her books. Carefully she shook out each dress or blouse or sweater. "You're as good as a lady's maid, the way you take care of my clothes," Mother used to say gaily when Mary Brooke hung up the dresses she had flung every which way.

The closet of the blue room was a spacious one. It would have to be to have held all Mother's clothes. Mary Brooke couldn't imagine Mother, even as a little girl, without lots of clothes, clothes of the sort she loved: fluffy, beruffled, and brightly colored. "Do try this on," Mother used to urge on those rare occasions when, of a sudden, she would take a notion that Mary Brooke too should have something new to wear. But the "this" was invariably too frilly, the skirt too full, the color so vivid that Mary Brooke seemed to fade inside it and become invisible.

Plain clothes are best for plain people, Mary Brooke thought as she hung a skirt in the closet.


After supper—which was something Aunt Olive called Welsh rabbit, though where the rabbit was Mary Brooke couldn't imagine as she dutifully ate what seemed to be a cheesy sauce on toast—Mary Brooke wished they might have built a fire in the stone-arched fireplace of the large dark living room Aunt Olive showed her. But Aunt Olive was occupied in pointing out what she must not touch, which was almost everything in the room.

"These," Aunt Olive was saying, "are Father's, your grandfather's, porcelains."

Mary Brooke peered into the dim recesses of a cabinet filled with bowls and plates, some of them small enough to be dishes for dolls, if Mary Brooke still played with dolls, which she did not.

"On no account," Aunt Olive said, "is this cabinet to be opened. In any case, I have the key. But I want you to remember that these porcelains are very, very precious. My father spent a lifetime collecting them, and each is worth a great deal of money. They are not playthings."

"I won't *touch* them," said Mary Brooke. Aunt Olive needn't talk to her as though she were a baby. Mary Brooke was careful of things. Everyone who knew her knew that. But then, Aunt Olive didn't know her, she remembered. Not really.

Mary Brooke sank into the large plush chair nearest the empty fireplace while Aunt Olive rubbed furiously at the glass of the cabinet front with her handkerchief. "That Harriet," she was muttering. "When that woman says 'a lick and a promise,' it's not just a figure of speech. And the antimacassars—," she said, turning toward Mary Brooke. She broke off, something flickering across her face; then, "We do not sit in *that* chair, Mary Brooke."

Mary Brooke found herself springing up guiltily.

"Why not?" she said.

"It was my father's chair," said Aunt Olive. She seemed to think no further explanation was necessary. "Be careful not to crumple the antimacassars," she continued, pointing to the lacy doilies on the chair's back and arms.

The house was not so big, nor had it as many rooms, as Mary Brooke would have guessed from outside. Downstairs were the living room and dining room, each dark and spacious with heavy old-fashioned furniture and a great many things Mary Brooke was forbidden to touch; the narrow kitchen where she and Aunt Olive had eaten their supper and silently washed their few dishes; the entry with its closet and gilt-framed pictures; and a long hall that led back from the entry to a tiny bathroom under the stairs and a small back porch.

Upstairs to the right was the blue room, Mother's room—my room now, Mary Brooke thought, though she could not feel that it was. The bathroom was at the head of the stairs, and across the hall was Aunt Olive's room. Aunt Olive opened the door and let Mary Brooke peer in. It was as different from Mother's room as Aunt Olive herself was different from Mother.

How *can* they have been sisters? Mary Brooke wondered. If she had a sister, Mary Brooke was certain they would be true soul mates—"as like as two peas in a pod," as people said about Mrs. Scherer's little girls. Mary Brooke had often longed for a sister, but always there had been only herself and Mother. "Just Mommy and her Brooksie," Mother used to say.

Aunt Olive's room was smaller and narrower than the blue room—this one should be called the brown room, Mary Brooke thought. The bed was small and narrow too, with a plain dark spread, and the curtains were white and skimpy, with cloth shades pulled down behind them. The furniture was simple, of some dark brown wood. There were a few pictures, also dark, and a desk and a straight-backed chair. *I* should like a desk, Mary Brooke thought longingly. She noticed there were no mirrors.

"I will show you my parents' room, so you shan't be curious," Aunt Olive said, leading the way down the hall. "I can think of no conceivable reason why you should need to enter this room," she said as she opened the door and stepped in. She flicked on the light, and Mary Brooke had an impression of an immense bed, of heavy dark furniture, of tightly drawn, slightly yellowed drapes. The room smelled closed-up and damp.

Mary Brooke nodded. Aunt Olive flicked off the light and firmly closed the door.

"That is all," she said. "Have you any questions, Mary Brooke?"

Mary Brooke shook her head, and Aunt Olive had started back toward their rooms when she had a sudden thought.

"But, Aunt Olive," she said, "this can't be all. There's the tower room, isn't there?"

"We do not use the tower room," Aunt Olive said without turning. "I told you that, Mary Brooke."


When Aunt Olive came in to say good night, she stood for a moment in the doorway before she left, a thin dark shadow framed in the light from the hall.

"This is your home now, Mary Brooke," she said. "I know you didn't particularly want to come here, and no one regrets more than I the . . . circumstances that have made it necessary. But we must make the best of it.

"You are welcome here, Mary Brooke. I want you to know that. Although I have never had children of my own, I have taught them in school for a good many years, and I daresay I know as much as anyone does about how to manage them.

"I do not know what Isa—your mother may have said about me . . . but I am—was—fond of her. I hope you will be happy here, Mary Brooke."

Quietly the door closed, shutting out the light.

Mary Brooke lay in the darkness, feeling small and hard in the big softness of her mother's bed. In the dark she could not see the blue spread, folded neatly on the boudoir chair near a window, or the shining satin drapes, or her reflection in the mirrors. In the dark there was nothing to remind her of her mother—nothing. So why this deep ache in her chest? Why the tightness in her throat and the prickling behind her eyelids?

It was the smell, she realized. The blue room smelled of Mother still—perfume and perspiration and cigarette smoke—that warm, intimate, *lively* smell that had been Mother's.

Mary Brooke squeezed her eyes shut, but a single hot tear escaped to puddle in her ear.

I shall have my *own* room someday, she thought . . . when Father comes.

# CHAPTER 2
# ANGEL-IN-THE-SNOW

Perhaps it was the quiet that woke her, or the light. It was as she imagined waking underwater might be—the hush; the diffused cold bluish light. Mary Brooke lay still, as she had learned to do when waking in a new place, and waited while her mind settled into her body, and bit by bit she knew where she was and why she was there.

At Aunt Olive's, she thought. In the blue room. Because Aunt Olive had finished with the "arrangements," as she called them, and had brought her "home."

The memorial service for Mother had been held in the Chicago funeral home where she had been taken from the hospital before Aunt Olive arrived.

The room at Mrs. Scherer's had been cleared of their things. Mary Brooke's had been packed into suitcases and taken to Aunt Olive's hotel. She wasn't sure what had happened to Mother's lovely clothes. She only knew that Aunt Olive had sighed when she opened the closet and saw them. There had been a disapproving look on her face, Mary Brooke thought, though what there was to disapprove of, Mary Brooke could not imagine. Mother's clothes had suited Mother exactly.

There had been debts to pay. (Aunt Olive had sighed again and looked disapproving, but she had paid them.) There had been phone calls to make and people to see and papers to sign.

During that time Mary Brooke had lived with Aunt Olive at the hotel. Although she was sorry to leave their room at Mrs. Scherer's—they had been there almost a year, longer than Mary Brooke could remember living anywhere else—she had rather liked the hotel. She had her own bed, not shared as sometimes she had had to share with Mother or as, when Mother was in the hospital, she had shared with Mrs. Scherer's girls. When Aunt Olive was away she had read quietly in the hotel room and enjoyed not having the noise of the radio or Mother's record player to disturb her. When she was hungry she was allowed to go down to the hotel coffee shop and order whatever she liked—"within reason," Aunt Olive said. Every day a maid had come in to make the beds and tidy up.

But yesterday she and Aunt Olive had boarded the train at the big Union Station. And now here she was, in Kirkland, Michigan, where she was to live with Aunt Olive—"from now on," Aunt Olive said, though Mary Brooke knew it was just until Father came.

From the brightness filtering through the blue satin folds of the drapes, Mary Brooke could tell she had slept late. But why was it so quiet?

Mary Brooke sat up and swung her legs out from under the covers. She slipped her feet into her slippers, which were lined up neatly beside the bed where she had put them the night before. She reached for her robe. It was too short and tight across the shoulders. Mother had been meaning to get her a new one—"when our ship comes in, love," she had promised. But this time, their ship had not come in. Mary Brooke jerked the robe around her and tied the sash. Then she went to a window, tugged on the drapery cord, and looked out.

The world was white. Lawns and walks and street could not be distinguished beneath the uniform blanket of snow that sparkled in the morning sun. There were tracks in the snow—foot tracks in a line to the front porch and away, tire tracks in what must be the street—but the snow was nonetheless unsullied, not ground to an oatmeal-colored mush or plowed into dirty ridges on either side of the street as it would be by this time of morning in Chicago. And that was why it was so quiet. Because this was not Chicago, with its rumble of trains, its squeals of brakes, its blaring of horns, its murmur of motors and voices and music, its rattle of garbage cans and barking of dogs. This was the sleepy little town of Kirkland, Michigan, on a Saturday morning after fresh snowfall.

As Mary Brooke watched, a calico cat daintily picked its way across the snow toward a bird feeder in the yard next door. She caught a flash of scarlet as a cardinal flew up at the cat's approach. The cat halted, twitched its tail—in disappointment, she thought—and changed its course.

Suddenly the back door of the house next door burst open, and a bundled-up figure in a red stocking cap and plaid coat streaked out, galloped across the yard, spraying snow before it, and tumbled backward full-length upon the ground. It lay still a moment, staring up at the sky, and then spread-eagled its arms and legs to make an angel in the snow. Mary Brooke shivered. She could almost feel the icy snow sifting inside her own collar. She watched as the figure carefully extricated itself so as not to disturb the angel and tiptoed away to survey its creation. She saw it nod, as though in approval, and then turn and tramp away around the house and out of her sight.

Slowly she turned away from the window and began to dress. That had been a child, she thought, one about her age, ten or eleven. Boy or girl, she could not tell, but . . . she stifled the hope that rose unbidden. Mary Brooke did not make friends easily, and there was no reason, she told herself, to think that, even if it was a girl, they might be friends. No reason at all.

The house was still silent. Mary Brooke opened her door. Aunt Olive's door, across the hall beyond the stairwell, was tightly closed. She tiptoed into the bathroom, where she used the toilet and brushed her teeth, hoping the sound of running water would not disturb her aunt. The bathroom was cold, colder even than the blue room. Mary Brooke buttoned up her sweater before she began to work the snarls out of her hair.

Mary Brooke's hair had been the despair of her mother. "I don't know where you get such *wispy* hair," her mother used to say, patting her own thick curls. But now that Mary Brooke had met Aunt Olive, she knew where she had gotten it. Her hair was just like Aunt Olive's, even to its indeterminate color, though Aunt Olive had hers cut short.

Still no sound. Mary Brooke crept down the stairs, hoping it would be warmer in the kitchen. It was not.

Aunt Olive had not forbidden her to cook. Mary

Brooke searched her memory thoroughly to make certain that this was not one of the many rules Aunt Olive had enumerated the evening before. But mostly they had had to do with being quiet and not touching things and answering when she was called.

Mother used to like for Mary Brooke to make breakfast. She liked to lie in bed and watch while Mary Brooke made the toast and scrambled eggs on the hot plate and perked the coffee. Then she would stretch luxuriously and pull on her gold satin bed jacket and lean against her pillows to eat the food Mary Brooke brought on a tray. "My little lady's maid," she would say fondly, smiling a sleepy smile. "You'll make Mommy fat, you know." She had always eaten every bite.

Now Mary Brooke found eggs and bread and milk in the refrigerator. She could not find the coffee, though there was a square tin of tea in the cupboard. It wasn't tea bags, as you got in restaurants, and Mary Brooke didn't know how to make tea from the crumbled leaves in the tea tin. Aunt Olive will have to teach me, she thought. There wasn't any cocoa either. She and Mother had often had cocoa, especially on winter evenings when Mother didn't have a date.

It was interesting poking around in Aunt Olive's cupboards. There wasn't, as Aunt Olive had said, much food in the house. Judging from Aunt Olive's thinness, she probably wasn't a big eater. There were, however, a great many dishes and pots and pans.

Mary Brooke chose two plates with a pattern of red and yellow apples and two small amber glasses for their milk from among the many in the crowded kitchen cupboard. She wondered why Aunt Olive needed so many dishes. Even when she and Mother were little girls, Mary Brooke thought, there were only four in their family.

She tried to imagine Aunt Olive as a little girl. With Mother it was easy. Just make her smaller and think of her morning face, before she put on her makeup, and take her cigarette away, and you could see her perfectly. But Aunt Olive . . .

Mary Brooke shook her head and began to whisk the eggs with a fork. This was fun, she thought, having a whole kitchen to work in. She and Mother had rarely had a kitchen—only those times when Mother had a very rich friend. Then they might live in an apartment or, once, Mary Brooke remembered, even have a whole little house to themselves. But it never lasted long. Mostly they lived in a room with, if they were lucky, a hot plate, as at Mrs. Scherer's, and took most of their meals with the other boarders.

The eggs were ready to cook, and Mary Brooke wondered if she should wait for Aunt Olive. She was awfully hungry herself. And would Aunt Olive want her breakfast on a tray, or would she want to come downstairs to eat? Somehow Mary Brooke couldn't imagine Aunt Olive eating in bed. In the hotel they had risen and dressed and gone down for breakfast in the coffee shop. . . .

Mary Brooke heard water running in the bathroom upstairs. Aunt Olive was up! She decided to set their places at the kitchen table. She poured milk into the amber glasses and found butter and marmalade. Then she put the bread into the toaster and melted some of the butter in a small frying pan. The heat from the electric burner felt good on her hands. . . .

"Good morning, Mary Brooke."

18

Aunt Olive came into the kitchen. She was dressed, Mary Brooke saw, in slacks and a sweater and low-heeled shoes. She was rubbing her arms.

"It snowed in the night," she said. "I've turned up the heat. . . . Why, Mary Brooke, you're fixing breakfast. . . ."

Mary Brooke was glad Aunt Olive wasn't angry. In fact, she seemed pleased.

"I always fixed breakfast for Mother," Mary Brooke said.

The pleased look froze on Aunt Olive's face.

"It is not necessary to wait on *me* as you waited on your mother," she said shortly.

"I only thought—," said Mary Brooke.

"In future, I think I should do the cooking," said Aunt Olive. "You may help, of course, and I will expect you to clear the table and dry dishes."

"Yes, Aunt Olive," said Mary Brooke, not knowing whether she should cook the eggs or not.

The toast popped up.

"You may butter our toast, Mary Brooke," Aunt Olive said, tying on an apron. She took the bowl of eggs from Mary Brooke's hand and poured them into the hot pan. "And Mary Brooke, be so good as to fill that teakettle," she said.

After breakfast, Aunt Olive got a pencil and a small tablet of paper and made a grocery list.

"I suppose you'll want some sort of breakfast cereal," she said, and it sounded to Mary Brooke like an accusation.

"I don't care," said Mary Brooke.

Aunt Olive sighed and made a notation on her list.

"What else do children like to eat?" said Aunt Olive. "Peanut butter, I suppose, and cookies and . . . Would you like some cocoa, Mary Brooke?"

"I don't care," said Mary Brooke.


Aunt Olive's gray Buick was in the small garage behind the house.

Mary Brooke waited while Aunt Olive slowly backed the car out, the tires crunching on the snow. Then she pulled down the garage door by its rope and climbed into the front seat beside her aunt. They backed down the long narrow driveway and into the snowy street.

Mary Brooke searched the yard of the house next door as they drove past, hoping to see the red-capped figure she had watched playing in the snow. They were almost past the house when she happened to glance up at a second-story window. A face was pressed to it, the nose flattened against the pane. Mary Brooke could make out only that it *was* a face, crowned with yellow hair.

"Who lives there?" she asked, pointing.

Aunt Olive glanced away from the street for a moment, following Mary Brooke's finger with her eyes.

"The Kohlers," she said. "Very nice people, though their little boy is entirely too rambunctious."

A boy.

"Oh," said Mary Brooke.

There was absolutely no reason to feel disappointed, she thought. No reason at all.

# CHAPTER 3
# ROOM 13

Starting a new school, like moving, was something Mary Brooke had done many times. She didn't feel nervous, she told herself, only a little excited. She was good at school. Teachers always liked her, even if kids didn't, because she sat quietly in her seat and raised her hand often with the correct answers and turned in her work, neatly done and on time, and never, ever caused trouble.

She and Aunt Olive drove to school on Monday in the Buick, early because Aunt Olive had to get there to prepare her classroom and find out what the substitute teacher had done in her absence. "And it will give us time to register you," Aunt Olive said, "and make certain everything is in order."

"Who will by my teacher?" Mary Brooke wanted to know. She had taken off her mitten and was stroking the gray plush upholstery of the automobile seat. She liked this riding about in a car. Mother had never owned one, though it had been a dream of hers.

But Aunt Olive didn't know about her teacher. "You will most likely be assigned to whichever fifth grade has the fewest students," she said. Aunt Olive taught seventh grade. "In any case," she said, "even when you are in seventh grade, it wouldn't be appropriate for you to be in my class."

Mary Brooke didn't say out loud what she was thinking—that she was glad she wouldn't be in Aunt Olive's class but that, anyway, by the time she was in seventh grade her father would have come to take her away.

Stroking the seat, she fell quiet for the rest of the drive and looked out the car windows. She liked this neighborhood, she thought, with its respectable brick and stone and stucco houses and neatly shoveled walks and snowy lawns. It was neither old and shabby nor new and raw-looking as their Chicago neighborhoods had seemed to be. I imagine Father lives in a neighborhood like this one, Mary Brooke thought.

The school, however, was a disappointment. It *was* new—one-storied and graceless, with big aluminum-framed windows and a flat roof. It was not Mary Brooke's idea of a school at all—no warm brick walls and echoing stairwells and halls that smelled of tuna-fish sandwiches and tennis shoes and chalk. This school smelled new and felt too—glary, Mary Brooke thought as she and Aunt Olive walked through the wide front doors into a shiny-floored hallway. In the glass-fronted cases along the walls were trophies and poster-painted artwork and crooked pottery glazed in bright colors.

"Wait here, Mary Brooke," Aunt Olive said, leading her through a door marked Office. The office had big windows looking out into the hall and a long, light-colored counter, behind which were a couple of desks and chairs and a great many filing cabinets. At the end of the room were two doors with signs on them. Aunt Olive knocked on one of these and went in when a voice answered her knock.

Mary Brooke took a chair where she could see into the hall. Not many people were at school this early, she saw. A janitor—Miss Osgood had said they should call them custodians; it was more polite—was pushing a wide broom over the floor. Mary Brooke couldn't see the point. The floor looked spotless. A woman, young and with bright red lipstick and a pretty, swinging coat, came hurrying through the front doors and toward the office. Mary Brooke scarcely had time to wonder if she was a teacher before she burst through the office door, pulling off her hat. Her high heels, which poked through openings in her rubber galoshes, made a tapping sound. She rushed through the little swinging door of the counter and dumped her purse and hat and gloves into one of the desks.

"Oh, hello. I didn't see you sitting there," she said to Mary Brooke as she stripped off her coat. "I'm late as usual. Why can't I seem to get here on time? Is Mrs. Brunskill here? Or perhaps you don't know Mrs. Brunskill? I don't know *you*, do I? Are you new?"

Mary Brooke felt a little dazed by all the questions. She could only remember the last one, so she answered it.

"Yes," she said. "I'm new. My aunt's talking to Mrs. . . . Brunskill, I think. She went in there."

She pointed to the door.

The young woman nodded.

"Well, then, that's all right," she said. "You're being

taken care of. I'm Mrs. Field, the secretary. I'm sorry I wasn't here to greet you when you arrived. Welcome to Forest Lake School. . . . Have I forgotten your name already? Or did you tell me?"

"Mary Brooke Edwards," Mary Brooke said.

"Welcome, Mary. I'm glad your mother found Mrs. Brunskill okay."

"Mary Brooke," Mary Brooke corrected her. "And she's my aunt, my aunt Olive, not my . . . mother."

"Oh!" Mrs. Field whirled from the cupboard where she was hanging her coat. She looked dismayed. "Oh, you're *Olive Brooke's* niece."

Tap, tap, tap, just as quickly as she had burst into the office, Mrs. Field came hurrying from behind the counter. She grabbed Mary Brooke's hand and looked earnestly into her eyes.

"Oh, Mary, I *am* sorry about your mother. If you have any trouble, any problems at all here at school, you just come to me, you hear? This is a wonderful school, really it is. And we all think so much of Miss Brooke. And we hope you'll like Kirkland and Forest Lake and . . . and just everything!"

Mary Brooke nodded, suddenly unable to speak. Please don't be kind, she thought frantically. Please, please don't say anything more! Did everyone here know about her mother? Was everyone going to talk about it and pretend to be sorry and make her feel . . . awkward?

"Good morning, Mrs. Field," said a voice from the door at the end of the office. It had opened, and Aunt Olive was coming out, followed by a tall woman in a brown tweed suit. The woman came toward Mary Brooke, holding out her hand.

"Mary Brooke, I am Mrs. Brunskill, the principal here at Forest Lake School."

Mrs. Brunskill shook hands with Mary Brooke just as though she were an adult.

"I imagine you might like to see your classroom and meet your teacher," she said.

She turned to Aunt Olive. "Miss Brooke, would you like . . ."

Mary Brooke thought Aunt Olive flushed. She was fumbling with her handbag, and her voice was low and hurried.

"I really do have to be getting along to my classroom," she said. "I wonder if Mrs. Field . . ."

"I'll be glad to take her myself," said Mrs. Brunskill.

Aunt Olive shot her a grateful glance.

Grateful for what? Mary Brooke wondered, but "I'll see you after school, Mary Brooke," her aunt was saying, still in that low and hurried voice.

"You may come to my room, room sixteen in the upper-grade hall. Just ask someone to show you the way. I leave her in your hands, Mrs. Brunskill."

Being left in someone's hands made Mary Brooke feel rather like a package, but as they walked to the classroom, Mrs. Brunskill talked to her the same way she had shaken her hand—as though she were speaking to a grown-up. She told her that her records had come from her old school, that it was a pleasure to see such excellent grades, that her teacher had sent along some favorable comments on her sense of responsibility and potential.

Miss Osgood, Mary Brooke thought. She would never have another teacher as good as Miss Osgood. Someday, if she decided to be a teacher, Mary Brooke thought she would like to be just like Miss Osgood, so refined. She hoped the new teacher would be a little like her—though probably that was too much to hope. Miss Osgood had been a better teacher than Mrs. Vanicini or Mrs. Deatrick from the two schools Mary Brooke had attended in fourth grade, or Miss Bradford in third. . . .

"This is your room, Mary Brooke," Mrs. Brunskill said. "Room thirteen. Your aunt's room is just down that way, on the right-hand side."

Thirteen! Mary Brooke thought with a sinking feeling. Thirteen was unlucky. And then she felt foolish. Miss Osgood would have called that silly superstition.

But Mary Brooke's heart was beating hard as she followed Mrs. Brunskill into room 13 and heard her say, "Mr. Henderson, I have a new student for you. This is Mary Brooke Edwards, who has just moved to Kirkland from Chicago."

Mr.!

Mary Brooke looked, aghast, at the man who was turning from the blackboard—only it's green, Mary Brooke thought with another jolt—to greet them.

An ugly new school! Room 13! A blackboard that was green! And a man teacher! Nothing was right here. Not a single thing.

Mary Brooke stood beside Mrs. Brunskill while she told the man teacher that Mary Brooke had come to live with her aunt. She handed him a folder and commented that Mary Brooke seemed to be a good student and that she was sure they'd get along just fine. Then, for a few minutes, they talked about other things—a teachers' meeting on Tuesday and something about a committee and the student council. And all the while Mary Brooke's mind was racing.

This can't be right, she was thinking. This *can't* be right. How can I have a *man* teacher? Men were apt to be hearty and loud as so many of Mother's friends had been. They liked sports and math, the two things Mary Brooke didn't like because she did them poorly. Men just weren't . . . quality, Mary Brooke thought. At least, most men weren't. She was sure her father was an exception, and perhaps her grandfather had been too, she thought, the image of that cabinet of delicate porcelains rising in her mind. But *this* man looked like Mother's friends, she thought. She could not stare at him, of course, to make certain, but from underneath her eyelashes, as she stood, head bowed, beside Mrs. Brunskill, she could see how big he was and hear his voice, which was as hearty as she had feared.

"Have a good day, Mary Brooke," Mrs. Brunskill said, turning away to leave her alone with the man teacher. "If you have any questions, don't hesitate to come to the office."

"I'm happy to meet you, Mary Brooke," said the man as soon as she was gone. "Your Aunt Olive and I have . . . known one another . . . for a good many years."

His voice did not seem so loud now, Mary Brooke noticed, and she dared to raise her eyes a little. His tie was crooked, she saw, and his suit was rumpled. He was putting out his hand, and though she shrank from it, it came to rest, lightly, on her shoulder. "I knew your mother too," he said, "many years ago. She was so . . . full of life."

Mary Brooke's throat was closing. No, she thought in a panic. Please don't. She felt his hand tighten slightly on her shoulder.

"I'm sorry, Mary Brooke," he said, and now his voice was so quiet that Mary Brooke could scarcely hear it.

Then, suddenly, it was strong and loud again. "But I am very glad to meet *you*, Mary Brooke, and glad you'll be in our class."

Until the other students began to arrive, Mary Brooke sat at the table where the man teacher had told her there was an empty place. That was something else wrong, she thought. Instead of her own desk, she would have to share a table with—she counted the chairs—three other kids! She looked through her school supplies and put them away tidily in the cubbyhole beneath the tabletop. She made sure that everything was in order, that she had plenty of clean paper left in her tablet, that her pencil was sharp, that her crayons were unbroken. And she tried not to think.

The man teacher finished writing on the board and went to sit at his desk, which was at the side of the room, near the windows, instead of in front where it ought to be. Mary Brooke had to squint to make out the words against the soft green of the strange blackboard. Her table was near the back of the room, and she thought about asking if she might move closer to the front so that she could see better. Usually teachers liked kids who volunteered to sit near the front. It showed you weren't trying to get away with anything. But since he sat on the side of the room, Mary Brooke wasn't sure it would have that effect, and she didn't want to call herself to his attention again. He might say something more about her mother. . . . Suddenly her heart was beating hard again. Oh, would he say something in front of the other kids? Would he tell them her mother had died, so that they would all stare at her and maybe act like they felt sorry even though she knew they really wouldn't care? Oh, please don't tell them, Mary Brooke wanted to cry, but she didn't. She just sat at the table and sorted through her supplies for the dozenth time and wished the day were over.

She was beginning to hear noises in the hallway—voices yelling and laughter and a scuffle of feet. By ones and twos and threes the kids began to troop in, greeting the man teacher as though they were glad to see him. Mary Brooke didn't look up to watch them. She kept her eyes on the tabletop or on her tablet, which she had taken out and opened to copy down the date the man teacher had written on the board—Monday, February 9, 1953.

The children were hanging up their coats in the long coat closet that ran along one wall. Mary Brooke's coat was already hanging there, where the man teacher had shown her, with her boots lined up neatly under it and her mittens and hat in its pockets. The children laughed and talked as they found their seats, and Mary Brooke wondered why the man teacher didn't tell them to be quiet. "Order, pupils," Miss Osgood would have been saying. "Let us behave like ladies and gentlemen."

These kids were not behaving like ladies and gentlemen, Mary Brooke thought. She saw a boy stick his pencil in his nose and waggle it back and forth. Some other kids were laughing, and a girl at the table in front of her said, "Oh, Shandy Kohler, don't be such a goon!"

Mary Brooke stole another look at the boy. Kohler? Wasn't that the name of the people next door to Aunt Olive's house? She wished she had seen what color hat he was wearing when he came in.

The boy laughed out loud and took the pencil out of his nose.

"Goon yourself!" he said good-naturedly, pushing

through the untidy arrangement of tables and chairs. He was coming toward her table, and—oh no! Mary Brooke thought as he plopped himself into the chair beside her.

"Hi," he said. "You new?"

"Yes," said Mary Brooke, not looking at him.

"Name's Shandy," the boy said.

Mary Brooke looked hard at her tablet page. She didn't answer. In a minute the boy shrugged and turned away.

"Time to get going, guys," said the man teacher and, miraculously, the room got quiet.

This was the moment Mary Brooke had been dreading. Now, in front of all the kids, the teacher would say her name and that she was new, and they would all look at her. This was always the worst moment, she thought. But never before had it been this bad. Never before had her mother just died. Never before had she been brand-new, not just to this school but to the town. Never before had she just come to live with her aunt, who taught in the very same school.

"Let's see who's here today," the man teacher said. "Is Ricky still home with the flu?"

"I'm here, Mr. Henderson," said a freckled boy near the front. "I haven't puked"—the children giggled, and the man teacher glared at them in what even Mary Brooke could tell was pretend anger—"since Friday, so Mom made me come to school."

"Clearly your mother's loss, Ricky, and our gain," said the man teacher, writing something in the roll book open on the desk before him. He looked up. "Did you know, class, that the word *puke* is one of those we call onomatopoeic"—he had gotten up from his chair and was writing the long word on the board—"because it imitates the sound it stands for?"

Mary Brooke was staring at the teacher, astonished.

She had never heard a teacher say a rude word like that one. Miss Osgood made any boy who talked like that go straight to the principal's office.

"Let's say it together, class, and listen as we say it. Doesn't this sound like vomiting?" the man teacher was saying. He was waving his hands in the air, as though conducting a chorus. "Pu-u-uke!" he cried, and the children shouted it with him.

"Pu-u-ke, pu-u-uke, puke!"

Mary Brooke stared about her, her eyes wide. She couldn't believe her ears. Everyone was laughing, including the man teacher. Then he returned to his desk, and slowly the room got quiet again.

"It is not, however, a polite term, class. I'm sure Ricky realizes this. We thank you, Ricky, for that lesson in etymology," the man teacher said. "Whoever isn't here, would you please speak up?"

Again the class laughed.

A girl raised her hand. "I think Wendy had a dental appointment this morning," she said.

"Thank you, Natalie, for reminding me. Anyone else?"

The room was silent.

"Well, then, I'd like to introduce your newest classmate," the man teacher said. He waved his hand in Mary Brooke's direction, but he didn't ask her to stand up as so many teachers did. "This is Mary Brooke Edwards, class. I hope you'll make her welcome."

Then he waved his hands again, as though conducting them, and the class sang out in unison, "Wel-come-Mary-Brooke!"

Mary Brooke stared at the tabletop.

She felt something poking her in the side. It was Shandy Kohler's elbow. She frowned at him.

31

"Say hello, dummy," he said softly.

Mary Brooke glared even harder, but then she became aware of the man teacher looking at her. He was smiling encouragingly, and before she even thought, she had said, "Hello."

"Glad-to-have-you-with-us!" the class said together to the waving of the man teacher's hands.

Then, "Enough of this frivolity, gang. Time to get to work," said the man teacher, and the worst moment was over.

# CHAPTER 4
# A DISCOVERY

She knew it was childish, but Mary Brooke delighted in the laundry chute. It was Saturday again—I've been here a whole week, she thought, astonished—and she was standing in the upstairs hall, dropping her dirty clothes, one at a time, into the small, high doorway in the wall.

Whoosh! went her underpants and undershirts. Whoosh! went her white blouse. Whoosh, whoosh, whoosh! went her socks and pink dress and corduroy pants. Mary Brooke imagined whizzing down the long tunnel of the laundry chute with her clothes, down past the first floor where another small door opened inside the kitchen pantry, and into the big laundry bin in the basement where Aunt Olive was sorting the clothes. Mary Brooke could hear the muffled thumps as the clothes landed in the bin. It's like a secret passage, she thought—when the laundry-chute door was shut it looked innocently like a cupboard—a secret passage for escape if the castle was besieged. . . .

"Mary Brooke!" Aunt Olive's voice, sounding hollow and far away, called up the laundry chute. "Mary Brooke, please come down here."

"Coming, Aunt Olive!" Mary Brooke cried, leaning her head into the hole in the wall. She bent to pick up the sheets they had stripped from the beds and dropped them down the chute. Whoosh! Whoosh! Whoosh! Then, regretfully, she closed the little door. From now on she could put her dirty clothes down the chute when she undressed each night instead of saving them up all week. Aunt Olive had forgotten to tell Mary Brooke about the laundry chute until this morning. It was there all week and I never guessed, Mary Brooke thought. It is a secret passage.

Apparently Aunt Olive's Saturday was laundry day. By now Mary Brooke had learned the weekday routine. Up early to dress in the night-chilled blue room—Aunt Olive said it would be wasteful to turn up the heat for the short time before they left for school. Breakfast in the kitchen, where the electric stove made a small oasis of warmth. The drive to school with Aunt Olive and the wait in the library until class time. (The library had been a wonderful surprise. Mary Brooke had never attended a school that had its own library. She had read three new books this week.) Then—getting through the day.

She tried to wait until just before the bell to slip into her seat beside Shandy Kohler at the table in the back of the room. She was the only girl at the table. "Keeps the boys civilized to have a lady in their midst," Mr. Henderson said. But Mary Brooke saw few signs of civilization. The three boys sniggered at everything and drew dirty pictures—Mary Brooke was sure they *were* dirty pictures, though she certainly didn't *look*—and shot rubber bands and spit wads and teased the girls with rude comments. They didn't tease Mary Brooke—but she knew boys only teased girls they liked—but it seemed to her a dubious honor at best to be liked by a boy.

What she couldn't get used to was the *noise*. Mr. Henderson's room was so disorganized, with people working on different projects at once. There were conversations in all the corners of the room—the mural painters at the bulletin board behind her, the science experimenters at the sink, the spelling group at the board, the readers with their chairs drawn into a circle near Mr. Henderson's desk. They all seemed busy and noisy and having a good time, which didn't seem to Mary Brooke quite *proper* for school. This week there had been excited preparations for a Valentine's Day party on Friday, with scraps of paper doilies and red construction paper littering the room. Mary Brooke had known *she* wouldn't get many valentines, though Aunt Olive had bought her enough to give to the whole class. And Mary Brooke was right. There were only twelve cards in her decorated shoe box on Friday—from kids whose mothers, like Aunt Olive, made them give to everyone.

Mary Brooke could scarcely think for the commotion in room 13. She longed for the tidy quiet of Miss Osgood's room, where everyone worked at once on the same subject, their desks in neat rows, and people only spoke when called on. A person knew what came next in Miss Osgood's room, but in room 13, anything could happen. The only thing Mary Brooke had found to count on was the half hour after lunch—sometimes it stretched to forty-five minutes—when Mr. Henderson read aloud from *Prince Caspian*. He didn't read so beautifully as Miss

Osgood, but he read enthusiastically, acting out the story, and the squeaking voice he did for Reepicheep made even Mary Brooke smile.

After school Mary Brooke would again wait in the library for Aunt Olive. Then they drove home, and Aunt Olive fixed supper and set Mary Brooke a chore or two.

"How do you like . . . Mr. Henderson?" Aunt Olive had asked the first evening, her eyes fixed on the slice of bread she was buttering.

"He's okay," Mary Brooke had said.

Aunt Olive had looked at her then in a—a *piercing* sort of way, Mary Brooke thought. But she had not asked again, and so Mary Brooke had not complained about the untidiness and noise.

After supper Aunt Olive corrected papers in her room, and Mary Brooke read or was allowed to listen to the radio in the living room if she kept the volume low. Then bed, where Mary Brooke comforted herself with stories in which she herself was the heroine until, at last, she fell asleep.

But today was Saturday. What, besides laundry, did one do on Saturdays at Aunt Olive's? Mary Brooke wondered as she trailed down the two flights of stairs.

Mary Brooke had been in the basement once before, when Aunt Olive sent her down for a jar of jam. She liked to think of it as "the dungeon," and it *did* look dungeony, with its narrow wooden steps and the great gray octopus of a furnace snaking its round arms along the low ceiling. The walls were gray too, which made them look rather like stone, Mary Brooke thought, and it felt chill and dank the way a dungeon would.

Aunt Olive stood by the washer, piles of laundry mounded at her feet, holding up Mary Brooke's pink dress and sighing.

"Your clothes are a disgrace!" she snapped without looking up as Mary Brooke came into the laundry room.

Mary Brooke didn't know what to say.

"*This*," Aunt Olive said, fairly hissing the word, "this dress is entirely unsuitable for school, even in spring, and it's only February!"

"The *middle* of February!" Mary Brooke found herself responding hotly. "That dress is okay." Mother had given it to her last May for her birthday, and it was one of the few that still fit. Even as Mary Brooke defended it, she knew she had never liked it. But *Mother* gave it to me, she thought, and felt her eyes prickle. "There's nothing *wrong* with my clothes," she said.

"Except," said Aunt Olive, "that you've outgrown most of them and worn out the rest, and a good many are in dubious taste."

"They are *not!*" Mary Brooke said. "Mother picked them out."

Aunt Olive looked up suddenly, peering over the top of her glasses. She sighed. "I might have guessed that," she said.

Mary Brooke glared. She could feel her heart pounding, and she knew she couldn't trust her voice.

Aunt Olive dropped the pink dress into the washer. When she spoke again, her voice had softened. "I think we'd better go shopping," she said. "That's what I wanted to tell you. Go change your clothes, and when I'm finished here we'll make a list."


Shopping with Aunt Olive always involved a list, it seemed.

Aunt Olive sat in the boudoir chair and asked Mary Brooke questions and made notes in her tablet.

"How many pairs of socks—*without* holes?"

"Your coat's too short, and this robe is worn to a frazzle. What about your dresses and skirts?"

"How many nightgowns?"

"Underwear?"

Mary Brooke fetched things from the closet and counted things in her drawers. She felt sullen and scarcely knew why she felt that way. I should be happy, she thought. It sounded as though Aunt Olive were planning a whole new wardrobe for her. Yet there was something critical about the way she did it—as though it were Mary Brooke's fault that she had outgrown her things . . . or Mother's. . . .

The department store in Kirkland was no Marshall Fields, Mary Brooke thought, feeling superior. It only had two floors, and no elevator or escalator—just a broad staircase. The children's department was on the second floor.

Mary Brooke was still angry, but she was beginning to be a little excited too. It had been a long time since she had had anything new. She wondered what Aunt Olive would choose.

But Aunt Olive, it turned out, didn't choose.

"We'll start with school dresses," she said peremptorily to the small fluttering saleswoman. "Please show us what you have in her size."

When the woman led them to the rack of dresses, Aunt Olive found a nearby chair and sat down.

"At least winter things are on sale," she said. "You may have three, Mary Brooke, or two dresses and a skirt. Which would you like to try on?"

Mary Brooke looked at her in astonishment.

"Me?" she said.

"Well, it's you who's going to wear them," said Aunt Olive.

One by one, Mary Brooke looked at the dresses on the rack.

"I'm afraid they've been picked over," Aunt Olive said, but Mary Brooke found a Dan River plaid in subtle greens and rust, a soft blue-gray flannel with a neat white collar, and a navy suspender skirt. None of them were the sort of thing Mother liked—no full, gathered skirts or brilliant colors or ruffles and crinolines. She glanced at Aunt Olive, and then she pulled from the rack a red corduroy with puffy sleeves that wasn't too bad. Perhaps if she took it, Aunt Olive might let her have a couple of the ones she really liked.

"These, please?" she said, trying to keep the quaver out of her voice.

Aunt Olive rose.

"The fitting room?" she said to the saleswoman.

In the fitting room Aunt Olive sat down again on the chair in the corner. As Mary Brooke tried on each dress, Aunt Olive looked at it critically, fingering the fabric and inspecting the seams. All of them fit, so, "Which three do you choose?" said Aunt Olive.

Mary Brooke swallowed hard and pointed to the red dress.

Aunt Olive's eyebrows rose.

"Very well," she said. "It's well made at least."

Something in Aunt Olive's voice made Mary Brooke say, "Don't you like it?"

"It's not a matter of what I like. So long as it's suitable for school and reasonably priced and well made, what I like does not signify. Do you like it, Mary Brooke?"

Mary Brooke stared at Aunt Olive.

"I thought *you'd* like it," she said.

Aunt Olive took Mary Brooke's hands and pulled her close. She looked straight into her eyes.

"Mary Brooke," she said, "I have said *you* may choose."

Mary Brooke's eyes dropped.

"I like the gray," she said, almost in a whisper.

"Well then, why didn't you *say* so?" Aunt Olive sighed.

It was Aunt Olive who found the hooded coat, brown tweed with gold taffeta lining. Mary Brooke loved it at once.

"May I?" she breathed, not daring to hope.

"I don't see why not," said Aunt Olive.


Riding home, Mary Brooke could scarcely sit still on the gray plush seat. She wanted to get home quickly so she could take her new clothes from their bags and try them all on again and hang them in the closet and fold them in the dresser drawers.

Two new dresses and a skirt, she recited to herself like a charm. A maroon sweater set and a new white blouse and a cream-colored cardigan. Three pairs of pants to wear under dresses on snowy days and after school for play. Three long-sleeved shirts that matched. A soft blue robe and slippers and two cozy flannel gowns. The hooded coat and a plaid head scarf. Brown rubber boots and a pair of penny loafers. Knee socks and bobby socks and new underwear. Mary Brooke had never had so many new clothes all at once.

Oh, I *wish* I could show them to someone, she thought. I wish I had a friend, or Father was waiting at home, or . . .

Mary Brooke remembered how she and Mother used to try on new clothes when they came home from shopping. Mother would show Mary Brooke how to walk with her pelvis thrust forward, like a model, and they would admire each other—mostly it was Mary Brooke who admired Mother—and Mother would laugh her wonderful laugh. Oh, I wish . . . , thought Mary Brooke, and her excitement turned to a lump in her throat. She stared out the car window, blinking hard.

But Mother never would have bought her so many new clothes. There was never enough money for clothes for both of them, and, "It doesn't really matter what *you* wear, does it, Brooksie?" Mother said. "You don't care." And Mother never would have let her pick them out herself. Mary Brooke tried not to think the disloyal thought, but there it was. Mother never would. . . .


While Aunt Olive fixed supper, Mary Brooke took her new clothes up to the blue room. With a small pair of scissors Aunt Olive had lent her, she clipped off the price tags. She shook out her sweaters. She folded her nightgowns and underwear neatly into her drawers. She rolled her socks in pairs. She hung her robe on a hook in the closet and lined up her shoes and boots and slippers on the closet floor. Then she began to hang up her dresses. She was one hanger short.

There were more hangers in the basement, she knew, but the basement was two flights down. I wonder if Aunt Olive would mind if I borrowed one of hers? Mary Brooke thought, starting out into the hall. But Aunt Olive's door was shut, and Mary Brooke couldn't bring herself to open it without permission. She glanced down the hall to the door of the front bedroom. I wonder . . . , she thought.

Quietly Mary Brooke tiptoed down the hall and opened the door of the room Aunt Olive said had belonged to her grandparents. The damp old smell of it filled her nose.

I'm not doing anything wrong, Mary Brooke thought. Aunt Olive didn't say I oughtn't to come in here, only that she didn't imagine I'd need to. And I *do* need to.

She didn't turn on the light. The hall light showed her the way to the closet.

This was a big closet too. It extended to the left of the door, and the long clothes pole was hung with plastic garment bags. The closet smelled of the plastic and of mothballs and old clothes. Mary Brooke pulled the chain that hung from a light bulb in the ceiling. The light came on, and there, at the far end of the closet, was what she was looking for, some empty hangers. She edged past the garment bags. The left wall of the closet was curved, she saw, like the curved wall of the blue room. Of course, she thought—it was the wall of the other side of the tower room.

Mary Brooke pushed aside the last garment bag and reached for a hanger, and as she did so she saw what she had been searching for since that first evening here in the castle. Low in the curved wall was a little door.

The door to the tower room!

# CHAPTER 5

# THE DOOR

But was the door locked? That was what Mary Brooke didn't have time to find out, for at the very moment she realized where the door led she heard Aunt Olive's voice calling up the stairs.

"Mary Brooke, supper's ready."

She did not dare to answer, for Aunt Olive would know her voice was coming from the wrong place. Hastily Mary Brooke backed from the closet, pulled off the light, and shut the door, making no sound.

"Mary Brooke?"

It might seem impossible to tiptoe and run at the same time. Considering it later, Mary Brooke thought so. But that is what she did, sprinting down the hall. The floor squeaked in spite of her.

"Mary Brooke, do you *hear* me?"

How could Aunt Olive help but hear *her*?

Mary Brooke ducked into the bathroom, flushed the

toilet, and then came out again, noisily, as she heard Aunt Olive's footsteps starting up the stairs.

"Coming, Aunt Olive," she called, trying to keep the breathlessness out of her voice. "I was in the bathroom."

Aunt Olive sounded cross, but unsuspecting. "In future, *answer* when you're called, Mary Brooke."

The problem was, when could she try the door? Mary Brooke puzzled about it all evening. Even after she had gone to bed she could think of nothing else—not her narrow escape or Aunt Olive's announcement that they would go to church tomorrow or even her new clothes. Unlike Mother, Aunt Olive never left Mary Brooke alone. When *would* she have time to try the little door?

Could she stay awake until the middle of the night— she felt wide awake now—then get up quietly and tiptoe past Aunt Olive's door to the front bedroom? As quickly as the idea occurred to her, she rejected it. Aunt Olive slept lightly. Several mornings she had complained that she "had not slept a wink."

I *could* just ask, Mary Brooke thought, and somehow knew she couldn't.

Church was not at all what Mary Brooke expected from seeing churches in the movies. (Mother had loved movies and had taken Mary Brooke often when she didn't have a date, but they had never been to church.) At Aunt Olive's church, there was no cross on the altar—in fact, no cross anywhere—and the priest or pastor or whatever they called him—"minister," Aunt Olive told her later—wore a plain gray suit instead of robes. He didn't even wear a backward collar. "You may go to R.E."—that, it seemed, was what Unitarians called Sunday School—"or you may come to the service with me," Aunt Olive said, once again letting *her* choose. Mary Brooke chose the service. She was curious to see what it would be like, and besides, she really didn't want to face another classroom full of children.

The service, however, was a disappointment. In the movies, there was always a lot of singing, kind of ethereal and stirring, but the songs they sang at Aunt Olive's church were mournful and slow, with difficult tunes and words about "peace" and "brotherhood" and "faith of the free." There didn't seem to be any prayers, though once everyone closed their eyes and sat quiet for what seemed to Mary Brooke a very long time. The minister talked and talked. Mary Brooke grew a little drowsy—she hadn't slept well herself last night—but when the minister said something about people looking within themselves for the answers to their problems, suddenly Mary Brooke had a plan.

"Aunt Olive," said Mary Brooke at breakfast Monday morning—she had decided to wait until then to ask because grown-ups were more apt to say yes if they were feeling rushed—"Aunt Olive, I'm getting tired of waiting for you every day after school. Couldn't I come on home today? I know the way, and I can walk with Shandy Kohler." Mary Brooke had no intention of walking with Shandy Kohler, but she thought that might set Aunt Olive's mind at ease about her maybe getting lost.

Aunt Olive drained the last of her orange juice and dabbed at her lips with a napkin. The place between her eyes puckered in a frown.

"I don't like the idea of children being home without supervision," she said. "What if there were an emergency?"

Mary Brooke had thought of that.

"Mrs. Kohler is just next door," she said. "You could leave me the number of school. I could come on home and change into my play clothes and just read or something." Mary Brooke had a sudden inspiration. "You could write down my chores, and I could do them. I could turn up the heat, so the house would be warm when you got home, and do up the breakfast dishes. . . ."

Aunt Olive's frown was deepening, and Mary Brooke realized she was on the wrong track.

"Or . . . or I could go out and play with the other kids?" she ventured, watching her aunt closely.

Aunt Olive pushed back her chair, and Mary Brooke sprang up and began clearing the dishes from the table. She couldn't see Aunt Olive's face, but it seemed to her that something had sparked in her eyes when Mary Brooke said "play."

"Everyone's always gone inside by the time you and I get home," she said to Aunt Olive's back.

"I suppose I *could* put a key on a string for you to wear around your neck . . . ," Aunt Olive said thoughtfully, and Yes, yes! Mary Brooke shouted inside herself, hope rising and fluttering in her chest.

"Get your coat on, Mary Brooke," Aunt Olive said briskly. "We're late, and I have a hundred things to do before class."

All the way to school Aunt Olive frowned through the misted windshield, hunched over the steering wheel, as she said things like "Absolutely no other children are to be in the house when I'm not home" and "You must remember to change your clothes before you go out to play" and "The numbers of the fire and police stations are right by the phone."

Mary Brooke said, "Yes, Aunt Olive. I will, Aunt Olive. I know, Aunt Olive."

At school Mary Brooke went with Aunt Olive to her seventh-grade classroom. While Mary Brooke waited, standing beside Aunt Olive's tidy desk, Aunt Olive wrote the school's phone number on a piece of paper and strung yarn through an extra key.

Aunt Olive's classroom reminded Mary Brooke of Miss Osgood's, with its neat rows of tables and uncluttered counters and shining clean chalkboard. Aunt Olive's desk was at the front of the room where it belonged; Mary Brooke felt a pang of longing for such order.

"Wear this under your dress," Aunt Olive said, "and don't go showing it to the other children."

"I won't, Aunt Olive." Mary Brooke was having a hard time keeping her mouth in a prim line. She clutched her hands together in front of her to keep them still.

"I imagine it does get lonely, sitting in the library every afternoon," Aunt Olive said as she hung the key around Mary Brooke's neck.

Mary Brooke nodded, biting her lower lip to keep from saying that nothing could be further from lonely than the library with its hundreds of books.

"When you get home, put this by the phone," Aunt Olive said, handing her the phone number. "Don't lose it now."

"I won't. Thank you, Aunt Olive."

Aunt Olive put her hand on Mary Brooke's shoulder and looked into her eyes until Mary Brooke had to look back.

"I am trusting you, Mary Brooke," she said.

Mary Brooke nodded, feeling her heart skip a beat. She forced herself to look steadily back at Aunt Olive, but a kind of sick feeling rose in her stomach as she said, "I'll be good."

47

Aunt Olive nodded, releasing her, and Mary Brooke fled to the sanctuary of the library to wait for the warning bell.

Mary Brooke was in a tremble of excitement all day. For once the chaos of room 13 didn't bother her. She scarcely heard it. In fact, one time when Mr. Henderson called on her she didn't have the faintest notion what he had asked. She looked at him blankly when she realized he had said her name. It seemed to her the room was oddly silent as he waited for her answer. Then someone tittered.

"Please stay in a moment from recess, Mary Brooke," Mr. Henderson said quietly, and Mary Brooke heard Shandy Kohler mutter a sympathetic, "Aw!"

But I don't care, Mary Brooke thought. She knew how to close herself up tight against grown-ups' anger—and I don't even *like* recess, Mary Brooke thought.

"Natalie, what do *you* think?" Mr. Henderson said, and of course Natalie Quinn jumped right up and started spouting off like the know-it-all she was.

Mary Brooke put her hand on her chest and felt the outline of the house key beneath her dress. The door to the tower room will be open, she thought. I know it will. She counted in her mind. Two hours from the time school let out until Aunt Olive usually came home. Taking away time to walk home and change her clothes, she'd probably still have an hour and a half to explore the tower room!

"Problems, Mary Brooke?" Mr. Henderson said at recess time.

Mary Brooke didn't look at him.

"No," she said.

"Sure?"

"Uh-huh."

She could feel his eyes searching her, trying to find out her secret, and the key felt hot against her chest.

"Okay," he said. "You can go, then."

Mary Brooke got up from her table and wandered toward the door. The truth was, she'd just as soon have stayed in, she thought. But then she'd have to put up with him looking at her like that—like she was a bug under a magnifying glass, and he was studying her.

At a quarter to three Mary Brooke had already gathered up her books and was watching the minute hand edge interminably toward the hour. It was taking forever, she thought, and was almost startled when the shrill jangle of the bell released her from her seat. She grabbed her coat and boots from the coat closet and ran for the door.

But once outside, she had to stop to put on her things. The snow was slushy and would ruin her new shoes if she wasn't careful, and the wind was cold. As she was bent over, tugging on her boots, she saw Shandy Kohler sprint past. The earflaps of his cap were up, and his plaid lumberman's jacket flapped open. Boys! Mary Brooke thought. They acted so tough!

I'll have to remember to wear pants under my dress if I'm going to walk home, Mary Brooke thought as she hurried along, the wind cutting at her bare legs. But her new coat was warm, and the hood kept the wind from her ears. Her boots made a sloosh, sloosh sound in the mushy snow.

Ahead of her, Shandy Kohler's black-and-red jacket could be seen in the midst of a cluster of plaid jackets. The boys were throwing punches and scuffling as they walked. Mary Brooke kept her eyes on the black-and-red coat. She *did* know the way, but it wouldn't hurt to be certain, she thought.

Behind her Mary Brooke could hear giggling. A group of girls were walking together, and Mary Brooke thought they might be talking about her from the way they were laughing.

At the corner most of the boys turned right, but Shandy and one other boy turned left. I would have known to turn that way, thought Mary Brooke. She was relieved that the giggling girls went the other way.

Now Mary Brooke's heart was beginning to pound with excitement. Soon she'd be at the castle. She'd let herself in with the key—she slipped her hand inside her coat to make certain it was still there—and then she'd change her clothes so that she wouldn't have to remember to do it later before Aunt Olive got home, and turn up the heat as she'd said she would, and then . . .

She hugged herself with anticipation, skipped a few steps, the snow spraying out beneath her boots, and suddenly realized she was alone on the sidewalk. Shandy Kohler's jacket had disappeared.

Her head swiveled, searching the sidewalks and street in a panic. A sort of smothery feeling came into her throat. Where had he gone? He'd been there just a moment ago, he and the other boy, ahead of her near that tall green house. Had they turned up the walk and gone inside? Had they ducked down an alley or cut through a yard?

Mary Brooke ran a few steps, feeling the slush slip

beneath her boots. I can't get lost, she thought. I can't get lost today. Not today when the tower room is waiting. Not today!

Then she heard voices—boys' voices, she thought—coming from the vacant lot beside the green house. She slowed her steps and tried to slow her beating heart.

I'm not lost. That's the vacant lot we pass going to school in the car. Don't be silly, she told herself. *Look* and see where you are.

There was the house with the yellow snow shovel propped beside the door—most snow shovels had red handles. And there was the house that hadn't taken down its Christmas wreath yet. Aunt Olive clucked her tongue every time they drove past it. "Probably still be up for Easter," she said. "Tch, tch, tch!" And there was the corner where they turned.

Mary Brooke walked swiftly past the vacant lot. She didn't turn her head, but she glimpsed a black-and-red blur from the corner of her eye—up in a tree. "Hey! You! Mary Brooke!" she heard Shandy Kohler's voice calling from the tree, but she didn't answer.

The castle was just around the corner, the third house across the street. She thought she saw the gleam of its weathercock through the branches of the leafless trees.

My lady, she told herself, your castle awaits . . . and the tower room!


The castle seemed entirely different when she was alone in it. The furnace made strange whooshing sounds—*ghostly* sounds, Mary Brooke thought—and the floors groaned. She thought she heard a knocking in the wall as she stole down the upstairs hallway toward the front bedroom. The door creaked when she pushed it open.

Mary Brooke tiptoed to the closet. She couldn't help but tiptoe. It seemed as though Aunt Olive might burst in at any moment, though it was only 3:30 by the little French clock in the blue room.

She reached for the chain to pull on the closet light and had a sudden panicky premonition that the little door wouldn't be there after all. "You have such a *wild* imagination, Brooksie!" Mother used to say—and I *might* have imagined it, Mary Brooke thought as she pushed past the garment bags.

But no, there was the curved left wall of the closet, and there was the door, not even so high as Mary Brooke's head. She put her trembling hand on the glass doorknob.

Why *did* Grandmother close off the tower room after Grandfather died? she was suddenly wondering. Why didn't Aunt Olive want to show it to her? What secrets did it hold?

The knob turned in her hand. She gave the door a push, and it swung inward. Mary Brooke stooped and stepped over the threshold and into the tower room.

# CHAPTER 6
# THE TOWER ROOM

In the wintry gray afternoon light that filtered through the window, the tower room looked small and dingy.

What was I expecting? Mary Brooke thought. Aunt Olive had said "a tiny unheated room." "We do not use the tower room," she had said. Did I expect it would be a real princess's tower, like in a book? Mary Brooke wondered, feeling angry at herself. She sighed.

From outside the diamond-paned window had shone, but from inside Mary Brooke could see how dull with grime it was. In the center of the ceiling hung a lamp, green with age and festooned with cobwebs. She thought it best not to switch it on. What if someone saw?

The curved walls of the tower room were lined with high bookshelves—if only they were filled with books! Mary Brooke wished. But they were not. They're only full of dust, Mary Brooke thought in disgust, wiping up a thick curl of it with her finger. A low shelf, wider than the bookshelves, ran beneath the window and was padded with a threadbare cushion, also gray with dust. Beside it, another wide shelf, this one table height, continued along the wall for a stretch of five feet or so. That shelf had narrower ones just above it. Beneath both the wide shelves were cardboard boxes. Maybe the books are packed up, Mary Brooke thought, dropping to her knees before one and tugging it out into the room. The box *was* filled with books, but—not wonderful ones, Mary Brooke realized as she leafed through the ones on top. *Porcelains of the Ming Dynasty* by Dennis L. Fugate, Ph.D., and *The Wonderful World of Ceramics* by Dr. T. Richard Suydam, and *The Art of Chinese Porcelain* by Robert Haldane-Bernard. They must be Grandfather's books, Mary Brooke thought, sighing again and putting them back. No stories, just dull columns of tiny print describing old dishes, and a few black-and-white photographs of plates and bowls and jugs.

That was all. Just a round, empty room with empty shelves and boxes of musty old books. Mary Brooke kicked at the box. What did you expect? she scolded herself. You're such a *kid,* still believing in magic. You ought to know by now that magic's just in stories.

Well, there was nothing to explore here, and nothing to do. Mary Brooke bent over and backed out of the door into the closet, giving the tower room one last, disappointed look.

It was only quarter to four. Mary Brooke got her library book and took it downstairs. Defiantly she curled up in Grandfather's chair in the living room and read for an hour, keeping her eye on the big ticking clock on the bookcase.

At quarter to five Mary Brooke closed her book. She

straightened the antimacassars on Grandfather's chair and plumped its cushions. Then she put her book away and pulled on her old coat—it was her "play coat" now, Aunt Olive said—and went outdoors. She had told Aunt Olive she would be playing, so it seemed best to be outside when she got home.

Mary Brooke had come out the back door. The yard was covered with dirty snow. Dogs and squirrels had wandered across it, and there were birdseed husks scattered beneath Aunt Olive's bird feeder, but the only human tracks were her own, where she had gone out at Aunt Olive's instruction to fill the feeder with fresh seed. She sat down on the back steps to watch for the Buick to pull into the driveway. The cement step was cold beneath her, but dry—Aunt Olive was careful to sweep away the snow.

From the steps she could see that the Kohlers' yard looked even dirtier and more trampled than Aunt Olive's. There was the place where Shandy had made his angel in the snow the first morning she was here, and his tracks ran every which way. In the front yard, she knew, were great bare patches, and his family of snow people—a big one with a man's hat and a pipe in its mouth, a middle-sized one with a scarf on its head, and a little one with Shandy's own red knit cap. But even Shandy's snow family was beginning to look shrunken and dingy—like everything, Mary Brooke thought, her chin on her hand.

Suddenly a cat came streaking up the driveway Aunt Olive shared with the Kohlers. In hot pursuit came Shandy himself.

"Come back, you dumb cat!" he was shouting. "Let that bird go!"

Mary Brooke watched with interest. It seemed to be the same cat she had seen her first morning and, yes, there was something in its mouth. It disappeared into the bushes at the back of the Kohlers' yard, and Shandy crashed in behind it. In a moment he came out again, rubbing his cheek. His earflapped cap was pushed to the back of his head, and his face was a study in disgruntlement. He was muttering. The cat was nowhere in sight.

Mary Brooke couldn't help but smile, and it was at that moment that Shandy looked over and saw her.

"What're *you* laughing at?" he said.

At what are you laughing? Mary Brooke mentally corrected him. But she didn't say it out loud. She could tell by the look on his face that silence was the wisest course.

"Stupid cat!" he said, kicking at the ground.

Mary Brooke couldn't resist. "It's a cat's nature to hunt," she said. "If you don't want her to catch anything, why don't you bell her?"

Shandy looked up. "Bell her?"

"You know, put a bell on her collar. Then the birds can hear her coming and fly away."

Mrs. Norton, their landlady before Mrs. Scherer, had belled her many cats, Mary Brooke remembered. "Gives the poor little sparrers a fightin' chance," she'd said.

Shandy's face lit up. "Hey," he said. "That's a great idea. Thanks. I'll ask my mom."

He was slogging toward her across the yard.

"Hey," he said again. "How come you didn't answer when I hollered this afternoon?"

Mary Brooke looked down at her mittened hands.

"I was in a hurry," she said.

"You're not very friendly, are you?" asked Shandy.

Mary Brooke didn't know what to say.

"I was just saying hi!" said Shandy.

"Well, you needn't make a federal case out of it," said Mary Brooke. "I just didn't feel like talking right then."

Shandy was standing by the steps now, looking into her face.

"When *do* you feel like talking?" he said. "You never say anything at school, and you sit right by me. I got BO or somethin'?"

Mary Brooke heard the sound of a car's engine and the swish of tires in the slush of the driveway. She jumped up, feeling relieved.

"My aunt's home," she said.

"Yeah," said Shandy Kohler. "Well, I was just tryin' to be nice to you like my mom said. Never *mind!*"

Mary Brooke watched him stomp back across the yard, slush spraying from beneath his boots. Aunt Olive had pulled the car up to the closed garage door. She rolled down the window and stuck out her head.

"Mary Brooke," she called. "The door?"

Mary Brooke ran to push up the heavy garage door. Shandy's voice had sounded almost . . . hurt, she thought. He was only being nice because his mother said to, she told herself. But he had acted like his feelings were hurt. What a funny boy, thought Mary Brooke.

The odd thing was, even though it had been a big disappointment, Mary Brooke still couldn't stop thinking about the tower room. Every day that week she walked home by herself after school—sometimes she saw Shandy Kohler, but he didn't speak to her again—and changed her clothes and read for an hour or so and then went out to wait on the steps for Aunt Olive.

"With whom do you play after school?" Aunt Olive wanted to know.

"Oh, just some kids," Mary Brooke said, a kind of squirmy feeling in her stomach.

"Well, don't let that Kohler boy lead you into mischief," Aunt Olive said. "I saw you playing with him Monday."

"I won't," said Mary Brooke, and *that* wasn't a lie.

On Wednesday it began to snow again. It snowed all night and all the next day and night. Once again, the world was . . . *pristine,* Mary Brooke thought, finding just the right word. She had discovered that if she dawdled a few minutes after the bell rang, most of the kids had cleared out before she started home. She didn't have to listen to their laughing and shouting or duck their wildly flung snowballs. Not that they would throw them at me *on purpose,* thought Mary Brooke.

She could walk home in . . . peace and quiet, she thought, her boots crunching in the cornstarch-dry snow. Sometimes she heard a squirrel chatter as it shook its tail at her from the top of a tree. Sometimes a cardinal cried its "pump-handle cry," Aunt Olive called it, though Mary Brooke had never heard the squeaking Aunt Olive said a pump handle made. But mostly, on those afternoons she walked home behind the other children, Mary Brooke had quiet to think, and what she thought of was the tower room.

I'm going to look again, she told herself on Friday, though she could not have said why.

This time the dimness and bareness weren't such a shock. It might be quite pretty, Mary Brooke thought, if it were cleaned up a little and things put out on the shelves and maybe . . . She rubbed her hand over the wood of the wide table-height shelf and saw that beneath the dust the wood was smooth and finely grained, a warm golden brown. If there were a chair, Mary Brooke thought, suddenly seeing how it would look, this shelf would make a desk. Her eyes opened wide, and her heart gave a jump. A desk! A desk of my own, thought Mary Brooke, and the excitement was bubbling up again. I could fix up the tower room, she thought. I could clean it and fix it up myself. It could be *my* room!

It was after four o'clock, but Mary Brooke couldn't wait to begin. She raced downstairs to the cupboard in the kitchen where Harriet, the cleaning woman, kept her supplies. She paused a moment when she had yanked open the cupboard door. Harriet's clean rags were folded neatly. The dirty ones had gone home with her to be laundered. If I use her clean rags, Mary Brooke thought, I'll get them dirty and she'll know someone besides her has been cleaning. But Mary Brooke had a whole stack of old, holey underwear upstairs. "Not good for anything but rags," Aunt Olive had said when they were sorting through Mary Brooke's clothes. Rags! thought Mary Brooke, grabbing the bottle of furniture polish and slamming the cupboard door.

An old undershirt made a perfect dust rag. Mary Brooke dragged a chair through the closet and into the tower room. Standing on the chair, she could reach the highest bookshelf if she stretched. She started at the door and began dusting and polishing the tower room shelves, from top to bottom as far as she could reach. Then she would move the chair and begin again. Dust, then polish, one shelf after another. Her nose itched, and she sneezed from the dust, but one by one the shelves were beginning to shine as her underwear turned black.

I can put *my* books on the shelves, she dreamed. But her own few books would take up very little space. When Father comes, he'll buy me books and books, Mary Brooke thought, forgetting that when Father came she would be moving again. I'll fill up all these shelves with books and pretty things of my own. . . .

A car passed in the street, and its headlights flashed through the tower-room window. Mary Brooke glanced at the window, startled. It was getting dusky and—how late *is* it? Mary Brooke wondered in a panic, jumping off the chair.

The clock in the blue room said five. Mary Brooke ran back to the tower room and dragged out the chair. Aunt Olive might not even notice it was missing from the front bedroom, she thought, but it was better to take no chances. She left the raggy underwear in the tower room but ran downstairs to put away the furniture polish. Harriet would never notice some of it was gone, she hoped. She was just closing the cupboard when she heard Aunt Olive at the back door.

"Mary Brooke, are you home?" Aunt Olive called. Her voice sounded strangely anxious.

"Yes, Aunt Olive. I'm here, Aunt Olive. I was just . . . just wondering what there was for supper. I . . . came indoors. It was too cold to play."

Aunt Olive came down the hallway, sighing.

"Good," she said. "It's just *frigid* out there. I was hoping you stayed in. I saw that Kohler boy outside, and he wasn't even wearing his cap, and I thought to myself that that child doesn't have a lick of sense. I can't understand

**60**

what his mother can be thinking to let him run around so. He'll catch his death of cold!"

Mary Brooke watched Aunt Olive pull off her gloves and hang up her coat and hat. She had a big pile of papers with her as usual, and an armful of books that she put on the little entry table. She sighed deeply as she bent to unfasten her rubbers.

"It *is* nice to come home to a warm house," she said, and as she said it she looked up at Mary Brooke, her cheeks pink from the cold, and smiled.

She's really not so *awfully* plain, Mary Brooke thought, surprised.

# CHAPTER 7
## TROUBLE SEEING

Now Mary Brooke's days had not only a comforting routine but a shimmer of anticipation. When room 13 was at its noisiest she could think of the tower room's quiet. When Aunt Olive wasn't inclined to talk during supper, she could review her progress in cleaning and plan the next day's work. Lost in Mother's big bed at night, she could remember that the tower room fit her—to a T, she thought, and it's all my own.

Weekends, especially that first one, dragged. But during the week she looked forward all day to the moment when the bell would ring and she could fly home, not minding anymore the laughter and looks of the other boys and girls.

Mary Brooke polished the bookshelves until they gleamed. I'm not going to put anything on them until the whole room is ready, she promised herself, trying not to think of how little she had to fill them.

Beneath the dust she discovered that the floor was

made of intricate geometric shapes of wood fitted together in a pattern that radiated from the center like a wheel. Opposite the door to the closet, the pattern was interrupted by a trapdoor with a metal ring for lifting it. Mary Brooke tugged and heaved, but it wouldn't budge. This must be the blocked-off door, she thought.

One day, when she knew Mrs. Kohler had taken Shandy shopping, Mary Brooke dragged the thin grayed cushion off the wide seat shelf and carried it out into the backyard. Sun and freezing temperatures had crusted the snow with ice. She crunched across it to the clotheslines, which were strung between T-shaped poles, and, struggling, managed to throw the cushion over. Then she beat it with the broom, making dust billow into the frosty air. Her feet slipped on the ice and sometimes broke through its crust, so that she found herself doing a sort of clumsy dance beneath the clotheslines—whap, whap, slip! Whap, whap, slip, and crunch! Whap, whap, whap!

The cold made tears in her eyes, but she didn't feel like crying. I feel like laughing, she thought, surprised, as she flailed at the cushion and sneezed with the dust. Her cheeks stung, and the cold fizzed in her lungs like soda.

When she carried the cushion back to the tower room and put it on the seat, turning up the side that had been down, she could scarcely believe it was the same cushion. It had turned a shining mossy color, and it looked soft and plump and smelled of the backyard hemlock trees, fresh and cool and green. Maybe magic isn't *just* in stories, thought Mary Brooke, smiling to herself.

She had to stack some of Grandfather's thick books on top of the chair to reach the ceiling lamp. She had found a can of metal polish among Harriet's cleaning things, and when she rubbed the lamp with an old pair of underpants wet with the polish, another magic thing happened. The crusty dull green lamp began to gleam with a rosy, coppery glow. She couldn't resist turning on the light, just to see how it looked, but two of the little flame-shaped bulbs were burned out. Mary Brooke couldn't imagine how she could get new ones. She had no money.

But money wasn't needed to make the window shine—only some ammonia in warm water and old newspapers for rubbing. Mary Brooke stacked Grandfather's books on the wide seat shelf—she took off the cushion first—and stood on top of them. They're good for *something,* she thought, wondering if Grandfather would be angry or glad to see how she used them. It was hard to rub in all the little corners of the diamond-shaped panes, but Mary Brooke hummed as she worked. Everything she did to the tower room made it more *hers,* she thought.

She pushed the chair up to the desk shelf to see how it looked, and sometimes she just sat at the desk, planning how she could put her pencils in a jar in that corner and her crayons there, just so, and her ruler and notebook . . . One day as she sat there, stroking her hands over the smooth desktop and down the wide facing of its front edge, she noticed there were two vertical cracks in the facing. She slipped her fingers beneath it and tugged, and a little drawer slid out. More magic! It was meant for a desk, she told herself. I didn't just make that up. It was *meant!*

She found the cleanest of her underwear rags and dusted the drawer. At its back something rattled, and she felt with her fingers and pulled out two paper clips and a penny, dull with age. There was also some paper, wedged into a crack at the back of the drawer. She worked it out, a yellowed, crumpled slip of newsprint. I need a wastebasket for throwing things away, Mary Brooke thought as her

**65**

fingers smoothed out the scrap of paper. It was something about a city council meeting, she read, and turning it over she saw that the other side was a picture. It had been torn, but Mary Brooke could make out some of the caption:

Miss Isabel Brooke, t
daughter of Judge T
Brooke, entertai
American Red C
Friday eveni
Civic Cent

Isabel Brooke. That was Mother, before she started calling herself Billie. When she was still Isabel Brooke, instead of Billie Edwards, Mary Brooke thought. She looked closely at the face in the grainy photograph. Yes, that was exactly what Mary Brooke imagined Mother had looked like when she was young. So beautiful! With her shining curly hair and her cherry lips—the picture was black and white, of course, but Mary Brooke could imagine Mother's vivid lipstick—and her laughing blue eyes. She was singing into a funny, old-fashioned microphone, and her dress had wide shoulders like dresses in old movies. That was what Mother had always said she was, when people asked. "I'm a singer," she always said, though Mary Brooke couldn't remember her ever singing anywhere but at home to Mary Brooke. . . .

Suddenly Mary Brooke couldn't see the picture anymore. Her hands, which held the clipping smoothed out on the desk before her, were shaking and her chest was heaving with hard, gasping sobs. Mary Brooke put down her head and wept.

* * *

Grandfather, or someone, had cut that picture out of the newspaper and put it in the secret desk drawer for safekeeping, Mary Brooke thought that night as she lay sleepless in Mother's bed. Someone was proud of Mother, she thought. Not just admiring and possessive, like the men friends. Not disapproving, like Mrs. Scherer and Aunt Olive. Not a little embarrassed . . . Mary Brooke's throat tightened as she made herself admit that sometimes she *had* been a little embarrassed by the way Mother acted. But *someone* had been proud, proud enough to keep that clipping from the paper and maybe take it out from time to time to look at. She didn't know why, but the thought eased something in Mary Brooke. Just a little. She curled on her side, her hands crossed over her chest, as though she were hugging the thought. She didn't let herself remember how it used to feel to lie curled against Mother's smooth warm back but just thought about Grandfather, or the someone, who had been proud.

"Mary Brooke?" Mr. Henderson said.

Mary Brooke jumped, startled. She had gotten so used to the way people wandered about as they wished in room 13, so used to Mr. Henderson, who rarely sat at his desk but moved all around the room helping whoever needed help, that she hadn't even realized he was standing beside her table. She looked up at him.

"Huh?" she said.

"Mary Brooke, are you having difficulty seeing the board?" He was frowning.

Mary Brooke hung her head. She had been squinting and craning her neck to try to make out the assignment written on the board, she realized.

"I'm used to a *black*board," she said. "Black is easier to see the writing on." That sentence was all wrong, she thought. Miss Osgood would have been horrified, but Mary Brooke felt so flustered she couldn't think how to fix it.

"Hmm," said Mr. Henderson. "The green boards are *supposed* to be easier on your eyes, but . . . Let's do a little experiment. Move up to that table, with Darlene and Wendy, and see how you do there."

Mary Brooke looked at him again. Did he mean move for good or just for now?

"Just for a minute," he said, as though reading her mind. "I want to see if it's easier for you to see the board from there."

Mary Brooke moved up, feeling self-conscious. Although everyone *seemed* intent on their work, she was sure they were watching. She heard the girls who were at the back counter, planting seeds in paper cups, giggle. They were probably laughing at her.

"Now," said Mr. Henderson. "How's that?"

Wendy stopped writing in her notebook and looked at Mary Brooke. She didn't smile or say anything, just looked. "Fine," said Mary Brooke. "This is fine."

"Read what it says," said Mr. Henderson.

"Green social studies book, pages thirty . . . four . . . to . . ." Mary Brooke tried not to squint.

"That's enough," said Mr. Henderson. "Now try from the front table."

Once more Mary Brooke pushed back her chair and stumbled through room 13's disarray, this time to the table closest to the board.

"Any better?" said Mr. Henderson.

"It's okay," said Mary Brooke. Let me go back to my *own* table, she was thinking to herself. She had gotten used to Shandy and the other boys. They let her alone, and that was fine with her. "I can see okay from *my* table if I squinch my eyes," she said.

"Read what it says," said Mr. Henderson.

It *was* better from the front table, Mary Brooke had to admit, but that was where stuck-up Natalie Quinn sat with her best friend, Marilyn Morrisey. "If nothing more than note passing and giggling happens at this table today," Mr. Henderson was always threatening, "I'm going to have to move one of you girls." But he never did.

He never did till now.

To Mary Brooke's horror, Mr. Henderson was saying, "Would one of you girls volunteer to trade seats with Mary Brooke? She's having a little difficulty seeing the board, and I know she'd appreciate it."

Marilyn looked sidewise at Natalie. Neither of them said anything. Joann and Patty, the other girls at the table, stared down at their books.

"It's okay, Mr. Henderson," Mary Brooke said, her voice coming out in a whisper. "Really, it's okay from my table."

Mr. Henderson paid no attention. "No volunteers?" he said, his voice disbelieving. "Well then, *I'm* going to have to choose."

"Choose Patty, Mr. Henderson," said Natalie. "She won't mind sitting with all those *boys.*"

Mary Brooke shot a glance at Patty. She was a round little girl, who puffed when she ran on the playground. Mary Brooke had heard Natalie and Marilyn teasing her. "Fatty Patty," they called her, and "Patty's boy crazy," they said in loud, meant-to-be-overheard whispers. Mary Brooke couldn't understand why Patty was always hanging around them, begging to play, or to walk home with Natalie, or offering Marilyn the Twinkies from her lunch. Now, she saw, Patty's face was bright red.

"No-o-o," said Mr. Henderson. "I think *you* would enjoy sitting at that table, Natalie."

"Mr. *Henderson!*" Natalie moaned. "Not *me!*"

"Yes, Natalie, *you,*" said Mr. Henderson in a voice even Natalie Quinn couldn't argue with.

Natalie shot Mary Brooke a poisonous look. She gathered up her things, while Mary Brooke went back to get her own.

"Jeez!" muttered Shandy Kohler. "*Not* Queen Natalie!"

Mary Brooke almost said, "I'm sorry," but she didn't. She kept her eyes on the floor as she made her way toward the front table. Natalie jostled her hard as they passed.

"I'll *get* you for this," she said.

Aunt Olive was even more silent than usual during supper that evening, but Mary Brooke didn't mind. She was dreaming of how the tower room looked now that she had moved in her things. She had taken her books from the high shelf in the blue-room closet—she was glad now that there were no bookshelves in the blue room, for Aunt Olive would never notice they were gone—and had organized them by author's last name on a shelf above the desk. She had put her doll—it wasn't the kind of doll you play with but a slender Japanese doll for looking at that one of Mother's men friends had given her—on a bookshelf beside the door and had arranged her pebble collection at the doll's white silk feet.

Mary Brooke had picked up those pebbles on summer afternoons at the lake. Mother had spent a lot of time on her suntan each summer, but Mary Brooke got tired of endlessly basking. That was when she explored for pebbles— the special, different ones in pretty colors and unusual shapes. When she brought her finds back to Mother's beach towel, Mother would stretch languidly and open one eye. "Very pretty, Brooksie," she would say, handing Mary Brooke the bottle of suntan lotion. "Rub a little between my shoulder blades, would you, love? Mmm. That feels good!" Mother was like a cat in the sun, Mary Brooke used to think—soft and plump and silky. She almost purred when Mary Brooke rubbed her with lotion.

Mary Brooke was thinking of Mother and of those sunny afternoons as she chewed her last mouthful of chicken à la king, and she was thinking how the pebbles had made the tower room feel—odd as it might seem—as warm and shining as they were.

"How long have you had difficulty seeing, Mary Brooke?"

Aunt Olive's voice jarred her from her reverie.

So. He had told. He had run straight to Aunt Olive that very day and told!

"I don't know," said Mary Brooke.

"What do you mean, you don't *know*?" There was that accusing tone again.

Mary Brooke looked at her plate.

"Could you see the board at your school in Chicago?"

"Miss Osgood let me sit up front," said Mary Brooke.

"So your Miss Osgood *knew* you couldn't see well?"

"*Black*boards are easier to see," said Mary Brooke. "And Miss Osgood said ladies shouldn't squint, but have smooth, *tranquil* faces." Mary Brooke liked that word, *tranquil*. It meant "peaceful, quiet," the way Mary Brooke liked things to be.

"And she didn't tell your mother?" Now there was an edge to Aunt Olive's voice. From beneath her eyelashes Mary Brooke could see her disapproving look. Disapproving! Of Miss Osgood!

"She did!" Mary Brooke cried. "She did tell her!"

It was a trap. Mary Brooke knew it was a trap the moment she saw the look on Aunt Olive's face, the way her mouth snapped shut and something—was it anger?—flashed in her eye. It wasn't *Miss Osgood* Aunt Olive didn't approve of.

"I thought as much," said Aunt Olive, and Mary Brooke thought she heard something satisfied in her voice. "Isabel *knew* you were having trouble seeing, but she neglected to do anything about it."

"She was going to!" said Mary Brooke. "She was going to when . . . Anyway, glasses make you ugly. I don't *want* to wear glasses."

Again Mary Brooke felt trapped. She shouldn't have said *that,* she realized as Aunt Olive sighed and removed her glasses to polish them on her napkin.

"I suppose your teeth need seeing to as well," Aunt Olive said. "And when was the last time you saw a doctor? Did your mother take you for regular checkups?"

"Mother took *good* care of me!" Mary Brooke said. Something thick and hot and choking was rising in her throat. "*Good* care!" Mary Brooke cried, shoving back her chair with a screeching sound. She could scarcely get the words past the choking. "She was a *good* mother," Mary Brooke said. "The best mother in the . . ."

Mary Brooke had to get her breath. She couldn't breathe here in the kitchen, with Aunt Olive staring at her, her mouth open a little and the tip of her nose quite pink. Mary Brooke ran out into the hall. "In the *world!*" she cried, running up the stairs.

She loved me, her heart was pounding. She loved me. She did. She *did!*

# CHAPTER 8

# TEARS AND LAUGHTER

It had been several days since Mary Brooke had been in the tower room. After-school time had been taken up with appointments—optometrist and dentist and pediatrician—as Aunt Olive had threatened, and, of course, on the weekend she had not been able to slip away from her aunt. But the truth was, even when she had the chance Mary Brooke didn't go to the tower room. Suddenly she didn't want to be there, where the pebbles were. She didn't want to be in the blue room either, though she had to sleep there. Instead she spent the time before Aunt Olive came home curled in Grandfather's big chair in the living room. In the evenings she lay on the carpet in front of the old console radio and listened to "The Silver Eagle" or "Meet Corliss Archer" or "Father Knows Best" while she colored or cut out paper dolls of movie stars.

It was Aunt Olive who had spoiled the tower room for her, she thought, though she could not have told exactly how. It *was* Aunt Olive. Aunt Olive had hated Mother, whatever she might say.

"I'm sorry, Mary Brooke," she had said that night, standing again in the doorway of the blue room like a shadow. "I shouldn't have criticized your mother," she said. "It's natural that you should have loved her very much, and I'm sure you miss her. In fact . . . I miss her too, even though we didn't see eye to eye. She was . . . my little sister . . . something . . . bright in the world, and . . . and, I *am* sorry, Mary Brooke," she said, her voice breaking.

But Mary Brooke didn't answer. She made herself tight and hard against Aunt Olive's phony, sad-sounding voice, and after a while Aunt Olive had closed the door.

The optometrist prescribed glasses.

"Bifocals," he said.

"Only old ladies wear bifocals," Mary Brooke said deliberately, fully aware that Aunt Olive wore them.

"So do little girls who need to see their books *and* the blackboard," said the optometrist.

"I can see my book," said Mary Brooke.

"That's why the bottom part of your bifocals won't have any correction," he said. "You won't have the bother of having to take them off to read and put them on again to see at a distance."

"But I don't *want* glasses," said Mary Brooke.

"Thank you, Doctor," said Aunt Olive. She turned, and her voice was cool and firm. "This time you may *not* choose, Mary Brooke," she said.

It was Thursday, a week later, and Mary Brooke was walking home from school, wearing her new glasses.

Now, here, away from Aunt Olive and Mr. Henderson, she *could* take them off. She had been planning to do so all day, but—I can see all the little twigs on the trees, she thought, marveling at the pencil-thin lines etched in black against the sky. And the snow—she could see the lumpiness of the melting snow and the individual blades of grass sticking through it. I didn't know you could see grass blades from a distance, she thought. Grass had always been just patches of green or yellow or brown to Mary Brooke, unless she got close to it. And bricks—I can see the mortar between the bricks, and the roughness of them, and . . . A blue jay flashed ahead of her and lit in the branches of a tree. Why, he has white and black marks on him, Mary Brooke thought. I can see his beak and feathers!

Mary Brooke didn't take off the glasses. She wandered along, slipping once in a while on icy patches because she was not watching her feet but was gazing about as though the world were new. It is *new,* to *me,* Mary Brooke thought, and suddenly she didn't care how she looked *in* her glasses because—because I can look *with* them, she thought. I had no idea there was so much to see!

Mary Brooke's eyes were so fixed on distant objects that she was almost past him before she noticed Shandy Kohler in his red plaid coat—the squares of black and the squares of red aren't all blurred together, Mary Brooke realized—hunched over in the street. He was looking at something, she thought, probably something disgusting. She kept walking, pretending she didn't see him, and then she heard a sound, a sort of low moaning and snuffling. She glanced and saw that Shandy was squatting on his heels, and his body rocked back and forth.

"Oh, Perky," she heard him moan. "Oh, poor, poor Perky. Oh-h-h!"

Mary Brooke hesitated. "Shandy?" she said before she had even decided to speak.

75

"Oh-h-h!" moaned Shandy, not looking up. He rocked harder. "Oh, oh, oh!"

Mary Brooke walked out into the street and looked down at the thing at Shandy's feet. "Oh!" said Mary Brooke, and she knelt.

It was Shandy's calico cat, lying quite still. Mary Brooke could tell from the stiff way its legs stuck out and the blackish crust on its mouth that it was dead, even though its eyes were open. Its fur, which was usually so sleek and clean, was draggled and dirty. Shandy was touching the fur, trying to smooth it.

"It's Perky!" he cried, and Mary Brooke saw that his face was streaked and dirty too, and the edges of his eyes were red.

Suddenly Mary Brooke wished she couldn't see so well. She closed her eyes. When she opened them, Shandy was still trying to smooth the fur. His tears were dripping onto the cat, mixing with the dirty water from the street.

"What happened?" said Mary Brooke.

Shandy didn't answer.

She put out her hand and touched him on the shoulder.

"Shandy? What happened?"

Shandy lifted his eyes. He dragged his sleeve across his runny nose and snuffled, and, automatically, Mary Brooke reached into her pocket for a tissue.

"I dunno," he said. "Got hit by a car, I guess. . . ." His voice sounded weak and faded.

Mary Brooke had scarcely ever seen Shandy Kohler without a smile on his face, but now the tears just kept spilling over the red rims of his eyes. His mouth was trembling. Mary Brooke handed him a tissue.

"I had her since I was a little kid," he said, wiping his

eyes. "She . . . slept on my bed and ran her motor so loud I couldn't sleep sometimes. . . . I'd have to kick her off the bed . . . but she'd always be back, curled beside me when . . . when I woke up. She . . . she . . ." He hid his face in the crook of his elbow.

Mary Brooke could hear the shuddery sounds he was making, and suddenly tears were welling in her eyes.

"Poor little cat," said Mary Brooke, and she began to cry too.

After a while Mary Brooke pulled off her glasses and wiped her eyes and blew her nose. She handed another tissue to Shandy, and he blew his nose. Mary Brooke saw that he had stopped crying, but his face still looked moist and raw.

"What should we do?" she said.

Shandy hunched his shoulders.

A car swished by, veering around them and honking its horn.

"I need a box to put her in," he said, "but if I leave her here while I go get one, she's apt to get runned over again." He lifted his swimming eyes to Mary Brooke. "I don't want her to get *more* squished," he said.

Mary Brooke jumped up. "I know where there's a box," she said. "I'll be right back."

She took off running, her boots slipping in the slush.

Her hands were shaky, and the key kept slipping as she unlocked the back door of the castle, but at last it opened. Mary Brooke was halfway to the stairs when she remembered her wet boots. She stubbed them off, shoes and all, and ran upstairs in her stocking feet. She tore down the hall, through the front bedroom, through the closet, and into the tower room. Falling to her knees in front of one of the cardboard boxes, she tugged it out from beneath the seat shelf. She pulled up the flaps and dumped books onto the floor until it was empty. Then she was on her way back to Shandy, barely remembering to pull doors shut behind her as she ran, the box thumping against her. She was glad she had not bothered to pull her shoes out of her boots, for she could tug them on together. Halfway down the driveway she had to run back to remove the key from the door. Once she fell, wetting the knees of her pants, but she didn't crush the box. In a few minutes she sighted Shandy, still hunched in the street as another car swerved around him, spraying slush.

"Here," she panted, shoving the box at him as she plunked down beside him, and for the first time that afternoon she saw Shandy Kohler smile.

Mary Brooke supposed that Mrs. Kohler really wasn't pretty—"Frumpy," Mother would have said, wrinkling her cute little nose at Mrs. Kohler's flat-heeled shoes and bunchy flannel dress—but something in the way her gray eyes went moist with sympathy when Shandy showed her what was in the box, something in her soft exclamation— "Oh, sweetie, I'm *so* sorry!"—something in the quick embrace of her heavy arms, made her seem beautiful to Mary Brooke.

Mary Brooke's throat hurt with a sharp, hard pain as she watched Shandy and his mother hugging. She pulled off her glasses, which were steaming up.

"I . . . I better go," she said, turning to open the door. Her mitten slipped on the smooth knob.

"Oh, must you?" she heard Mrs. Kohler say. "You've been so kind to help Shandy bring poor Perky home. Can't you stay for a cup of cocoa?"

Mary Brooke hesitated. She didn't really want to go across the driveway to the cold, empty-feeling castle, but she didn't belong here either, in this warm, fragrant kitchen.

"My aunt'll be coming home," she said. "I think I better go."

Shandy's face emerged from the front of his mother's dress, where it had been buried. Her arms were still around him—protecting, Mary Brooke thought.

"Don't go, Mary Brooke," he said. "Miss Brooke won't be home till five. You've got time."

"I've baked some banana bread," Mrs. Kohler said, her voice coaxing.

"We-ell," said Mary Brooke.

"I'm through crying," said Shandy, wiping his face on his sleeve again—Mrs. Kohler didn't seem to notice, Mary Brooke observed. "Please stay."

That wonderful smell was the banana bread, Mary Brooke thought. "Well, okay," she said.

Mrs. Kohler spread the warm banana bread with cream cheese, something Mary Brooke had never tasted. It was delicious with the rich hot cocoa. Mary Brooke was soon full and warm and a little sleepy.

The food had made Shandy feel better too. He had stopped crying, though his voice still trembled now and again when he talked about Perky, who had been left on the porch in Mary Brooke's box.

"She looks so dirty, Ma," he said as he set down his empty mug. "Perky always kept her coat clean and pretty, but now she looks awful!"

"We'll clean her up," said Mrs. Kohler from the sink where she was washing the bread pan.

"Can we, Ma?"

"Of course we can. You run down to the basement and get a couple of those old towels from the cupboard and

Perky's brush. She'll look real pretty when we get through with her."

"Want to help, Mary Brooke?" Shandy said, already on his feet and halfway to the basement door.

Mary Brooke didn't answer. I wonder what it feels like to touch something dead? she thought. Back in the street it was Shandy who had lifted the cat into the box. Mary Brooke had only helped by carrying one side. The box hadn't been heavy, only awkward, and she had folded down the box flaps so that she didn't have to look as they stumbled down the street. Now she didn't want to look at the cat again, but she didn't want to leave Shandy's house either.

Shandy reappeared, carrying the towels and the brush.

"Where should we work?" he said.

"Why, right here, I suppose," said Mrs. Kohler. "Bring the box in and set it on the table. I'll clear the dishes away."

Mary Brooke jumped up and carried her plate and mug to the sink.

"I'll do it, Mrs. Kohler," she said, trying to imagine Aunt Olive letting anyone put a dead cat on her kitchen table.

Mrs. Kohler turned that beautiful smile on her, a smile that reminded Mary Brooke of Shandy.

"Why, what a good help you are, Mary Brooke," she said.

Mrs. Kohler closed Perky's eyes. That made it easier for Mary Brooke to look at the cat.

"I think she must have been hit early in the day," Mrs. Kohler told them. "She's so cold and stiff, it must have happened quite a while ago."

Shandy had tears in his eyes again, but he was smiling bravely as he toweled the wet fur dry.

"This is like a funeral home, isn't it?" he said. "Like we're the undertakers." He grinned suddenly. "Goodness, but the deceased is a mess, isn't she?" he said in a deep, solemn, undertaking voice.

Mrs. Kohler smiled. "One is just never at one's best dead," she said, and Shandy laughed out loud.

Mary Brooke was shocked. How *could* they be making jokes? she thought, frowning.

Mrs. Kohler said, "Mary Brooke, I suppose you'll need your box back?"

"Oh, no!" Mary Brooke couldn't put Grandfather's books back into a box that had held a dead cat. "No, you can keep it. It's okay."

"Sure?"

"Uh-huh," said Mary Brooke. "But . . . but shouldn't we wrap her up in something, inside the box?"

Shandy had reached for the brush and was smoothing Perky's rumpled fur.

"Yeah," he said. "Her blanket. We should wrap her in her blanket to"—his voice broke; he *is* sad, Mary Brooke thought; then can you be sad and laughing at the same time? she wondered—"to keep her cozy."

Mrs. Kohler had wet a rag at the sink. She was sponging the cat's encrusted mouth. Mary Brooke saw that the rag was turning pink. Blood, she thought, a sudden, terrifying pounding in her head. I need to go home, she thought in a panic, but she made no move, only knelt on her chair and watched Shandy and his mother make the cat—"Beautiful," Mrs. Kohler said, stepping back to view their work. "She looks almost her old self, doesn't she?"

Shandy moved close to his mother and gazed with her. Mary Brooke saw Mrs. Kohler's arm go around him, and then she felt Mrs. Kohler's other arm reaching for her. Mrs. Kohler drew her off the chair and to her side, and they stood, the three of them together, and Mary Brooke's throat began to hurt again.

"She was a good old cat," said Shandy. "A *darn* good old cat!"

Mrs. Kohler didn't even call him down for swearing, Mary Brooke noticed as she felt the squeeze of Mrs. Kohler's arm.

"Where do you suppose Perky is now?" Shandy wondered aloud as they sat together on his back steps, watching for Aunt Olive.

Mary Brooke shot him a startled glance.

"Why . . . on the porch," she said. They had put her, snugly wrapped in the blanket from her basket and nestled in Mary Brooke's box, back outside again—"So's she'll keep," Shandy had said, rather indelicately, she thought—to wait for Shandy's father to come home to bury her.

"I don't mean her body," Shandy said. "I mean her . . . I dunno, her spirit, I guess."

Mary Brooke shook her head.

"Maybe there's a cat heaven," Shandy said. "Full of birds to chase. Perky'd *love* that!"

"Not very nice for the birds," said Mary Brooke.

Shandy cocked his head to one side. He seemed to be thinking. "Yeah," he said at last, laughing. "I guess cat heaven would be *bird hell*, wouldn't it?"

Mary Brooke didn't know what to say. "How come you make jokes about it?" she said.

He looked at her, his face wrinkled in thought. "I dunno," he said. "You can't cry *all* the time, can you?"

Mary Brooke thought about that. She hadn't cried at all when Mother died, not as she had cried this afternoon over Perky, or as she had cried over the newspaper clipping in the desk drawer, or the other night, when Aunt Olive had said those things about Mother. But I didn't laugh either, Mary Brooke thought. I didn't laugh *or* cry, Mary Brooke thought, and Shandy had done both, all at once. Maybe it's different with cats than it is with people, Mary Brooke thought.

# CHAPTER 9
# FRIENDS AND ENEMIES

Hot lunch on Fridays, Mary Brooke had learned, was invariably "tuna surprise." She craned her head around the line of children in front of her to confirm this fact and was pleased that even at this distance, with her glasses, she could identify the gluey substance the hair-netted cafeteria lady was plopping onto held-out plates. Mary Brooke reached for a carton of milk, which she put onto her tray beside her library book.

At lunchtime Mary Brooke always sat alone and read her book. She liked to find a place at the end of a table, preferably of older girls. They pretty much ignored her, absorbed in their giggling gossip.

"Hssst! Mary Brooke!"

Mary Brooke had just decided to skip the pale canned peaches but take a dish of the rubbery pudding when she heard the whisper.

"Mary Brooke!"

"Hmm?"

She turned to see Shandy Kohler, his lunch sliding precariously toward the front of his tilted tray as he tried to attract her attention.

"Mary Brooke, I need to talk to you," he was whispering.

"Okay," said Mary Brooke, turning back to hold out her plate to the cafeteria lady.

As soon as the plate was filled with tuna surprise and green beans and a soggy-looking roll, each in its own little compartment, Mary Brooke followed Shandy across the cafeteria. Did the fact that she had helped with Perky yesterday mean that she and Shandy Kohler were friends? she wondered. He had never wanted to talk to her before. She looked around self-consciously. Fifth-grade boys and girls didn't actually sit together at lunch. Would the other kids notice and tease?

Shandy had chosen a table that was almost empty. At one end were two boys from the other fifth-grade class, but Shandy set his tray down as far from them as he could get. He was motioning frantically for her to join him.

Mary Brooke made her hesitating way toward him and set down her tray.

"What?" she said. "What do you want?"

Shandy had pulled out his chair with a scraping sound and plopped down. Suddenly he wasn't looking at her but was busy opening his milk carton and sticking his straw into it. He took a deep slurp of milk and said, out of the side of his mouth, "Sit *down,* will you?"

Mary Brooke sat down.

"What?" she said.

"I . . ." He looked over his shoulder as though afraid

**86**

someone were listening. "I wanted to talk to you about yesterday."

"Yesterday?" said Mary Brooke. She picked up her fork and poked at the tuna surprise.

"Yeah. I . . . I wanted to ask you . . ."

He certainly was taking his time getting to the point, Mary Brooke thought. She glanced at him and saw that a flush of pink was washing up his face.

"You . . ." Shandy put his head down and took another slurp of milk. "You haven't told anyone about . . . about yesterday, have you?" he said, still in a whisper.

Mary Brooke leaned closer. It was difficult to hear what he was saying, he was talking so softly and fast.

"About Perky?" she said.

"No, about . . . about me . . . crying!" Shandy blurted, looking up suddenly, his face intense with worry.

"No!" Mary Brooke said.

She could see the relief in his eyes.

"Oh, good! Uh . . . uh, would you mind . . . *not* telling anyone?" Shandy said. "The other guys . . . well, *you* know."

Mary Brooke nodded. Yes, of course she knew. The other boys would make Shandy's life miserable if they heard how he had cried over his dead pet. Though I don't know why, she thought. I bet any one of them would have done the same thing if they'd found *their* cat killed in the street. Still, it was lucky for Shandy that it was Mary Brooke who had seen him and not Ricky or Donald or Harvey Swanson. Especially not Harvey Swanson.

"I won't tell," Mary Brooke said. "You don't need to worry."

Shandy flashed her his radiant smile and tore off a huge mouthful of soggy roll.

"Gosh, thanks," he mumbled around it.

Mary Brooke began eating her own lunch. There didn't seem to be anything else to say. She wondered if it would be rude to open her book. She was dying to start it, a book so new that she was the first person to check it out. She smoothed its fresh plastic cover and read the title again, *Moccasin Trail*.

"Wouldn't sit with *her* if I was you, Shandy."

The voice rose out of the cafeteria hubbub, clear and sharp as vinegar.

Mary Brooke froze. She kept her eyes on her plate and lifted her fork, laden with beans, to her mouth. But she couldn't swallow the bread she was chewing. She put her fork down again and picked up her milk.

"Just ignore her," Shandy said in a low, sympathetic voice.

But the vinegar voice was continuing, rising even more shrilly, and it seemed to Mary Brooke that other voices were quieting to listen.

"'Course, you don't know what *I* know," it was saying, and Mary Brooke recognized it as Natalie Quinn's voice. "About her *mother*, I mean," said Natalie Quinn. "You don't know about her mother."

Her voice was coming from the next table, Mary Brooke realized, the table behind them.

"What about her mother?" came Patty's voice. "I thought her mother died."

"Died of *what*?" said Natalie Quinn.

"Just died, I guess," said Patty.

"It's really not very nice to talk about dead people," said another voice. Wendy, Mary Brooke guessed.

Mary Brooke was chewing and chewing. She took a sip

of milk, but it couldn't wash the bread past the lump in her throat.

Shandy turned. "Yeah, Queen Natalie," he said. "Dry up!"

Natalie Quinn acted as though she didn't hear him. "*My* mother says it's just a scandal," she said, "someone from Kirkland ending up like that!"

"Like what?" said Patty.

"I'm not supposed to tell," said Natalie, her voice sounding virtuous. "It's a secret, but if I was you, Shandy Kohler, I wouldn't have a thing to do with Mary Brooke Edwards."

Shandy was standing up now. Mary Brooke wanted to pull him back down into his seat. She wanted to tell him not to make it worse, but she couldn't with her mouth so full of food she couldn't swallow.

"Shut up, Queen Natalie," Shandy was saying. "You don't know anything!"

"I do too!"

"Do not."

"Do too!"

"Liar, liar, pants on fire," said Shandy.

"I know Mary Brooke's mother had an *abortion!*" said Natalie, the ugly word hissing out of her mouth like a snake.

"What's *that?*" said Patty in her clear, loud voice.

A hush seemed to have fallen over the cafeteria, Mary Brooke thought. Everyone was listening, listening to Natalie Quinn's voice that went on and on.

"It's baby killing, that's what it is. Her mother killed her baby and then died herself. It was her punishment, *my* mother says, and served her right!"

Mary Brooke didn't even realize she had pushed back her chair. She wasn't aware of standing or turning, but suddenly she was looking into Natalie Quinn's slitty eyes.

"My mother didn't even have a baby!" she yelled and realized that somehow she had swallowed after all.

"Well, of course she didn't," yelled Natalie Quinn right back. "That's what abortion is—killing your baby before the poor little thing is even born."

"That's not true," Mary Brooke said, but something red was rising before her eyes. "It's not . . . true," she said again, her voice faltering. "My mother wouldn't . . . do such a thing. . . ."

The red was all around her, pounding in her ears and blinding her. It was in her nose, so she couldn't breathe, and in her throat. She flung her arms wildly, trying to ward it off. She was running before she even knew she had to run, bumping into chairs and tables, upsetting trays. Hands reached to grab her, legs stretched out to trip her, but Mary Brooke evaded them all. She ran out of the cafeteria and down the hall toward the big front door. She ran and ran and ran.

It was the cold that brought her back to herself—back from the stifling red vortex into which she had been sucked by Natalie's voice, back from the pounding anger and the fear. Although the sun was shining, the cold stung her stiff wet cheeks and searched through her sweater and dress. She could feel hard little goose bumps on her arms and the tightness of her muscles bunched against the cold. She was running, she saw, toward the castle—from habit, she supposed. Her steps stumbled, slowed, then speeded again when she felt how slowing let the cold settle into her. She could feel her key knocking hard against her chest. Where else can I go? she thought. Not back to school. Not back to the horrified eyes of her classmates, the spiteful voice of Natalie Quinn.

It wasn't true, what Natalie had said. Mother was sick. She was sick long before the bloody night, the night Mary Brooke woke beside Mother with her legs wet and sticky-warm and heard the whimpering sound Mother was making in the darkness and felt the fever pulsing from her skin. Mother had been sick since "Uncle" Steve stopped coming around—it was Mother who had wanted Mary Brooke to call him Uncle. "Someday," she had said, "you'll be able to call him Daddy. When we're married. Then, you'll see, love, we'll be so happy." Mother's face had had that look, that shining, *hopeful* look that made Mary Brooke feel a little sick inside. It always came just before the bad times, that look. Mother just couldn't seem to *learn*. But Mary Brooke knew what was coming, and sure enough, "Uncle" Steve stopped calling, and then, right after that, Mother got sick.

Men had stopped calling before, lots of times, and usually Mother cried, and sometimes she threw things and yelled, or moped around for a few days, gazing bitterly into her drink and smoking one cigarette after another. But always before, sooner or later, Mother got over it. She'd wake up one morning and start putting on her makeup, and Mary Brooke would hear her humming as she fussed with her hair—"Get your hat and get your coat. Leave your worries on your doorstep. . . ." And maybe something Mary Brooke said would strike her funny, and she'd laugh. She'd hug Mary Brooke and swing her around in a hilarious, dizzy dance.

But this time Mother had cried for days. She sat at her

91

dressing table and stared into her mirror, her mouth twisted. "They're all alike, Brooksie," she said. "Just good-time Charlies! You seen my cigarettes?" And when Mary Brooke handed her the half-empty packet she hadn't looked right, her face yellowy and her hair stringy. There was a look in her eyes Mary Brooke hadn't seen before, even in the worst times. If Mary Brooke hadn't known better, she'd have thought it was a scared look, except what would Mother have to be *scared* about?

She wouldn't eat the good breakfasts Mary Brooke made for her. "Not now," she'd say, sitting on the edge of the bed with her head in her hands, and when Mary Brooke came home from school the plate would be there on the bedside table, the eggs congealed and the toast dry and hard. Mother would still be in her nightgown, staring out the window and smoking, and the skin around her eyes looked bruised.

That's what had been wrong with her, the sickness. Not what Natalie Quinn had said. Not Mother. Mother wouldn't do a thing like that. Mother was *crazy* about babies. "Someday, Brooksie," she used to say, "someday we're going to have a little baby sister or brother for you. How'd you like that? Your mommy a fat, lazy housewife, sitting around watching one of those new televisions all day. No more lousy waitressing jobs . . ."

Lies. It was all lies that Natalie had made up because she was mad she had to sit in the back of the room. What did Natalie Quinn know about Mother? Not a thing! Just lies.

Mary Brooke was fumbling with her key at the back door. Her fingers were so cold they wouldn't work properly, but at last the key clicked in the lock, and when she shoved against it the door opened.

After outdoors the house felt warm, but Mary Brooke couldn't stop shivering. Her teeth chattered so hard her jaw ached. Her head ached too, and suddenly she wanted nothing so much as to sleep. Wearily she pulled herself up the stairs toward the blue room, her feet cold and blockish in her wet shoes.

What was Aunt Olive going to say when she heard that Mary Brooke had run away from school? What would she do? She'd be mad, Mary Brooke knew that. She'd probably punish her. But I don't care, thought Mary Brooke.

The blue room felt icy. Mary Brooke couldn't bring herself to touch the cold blue bedspread. She turned away.

There was an afghan folded on the foot of the bed in the front bedroom. Mary Brooke had noticed it as she came and went from the tower room. It was yellow and rose and cream, thick warm colors. I'll wrap up in that, Mary Brooke thought, until I get warm.

But when she was in the front bedroom, the door closed carefully behind her, Mary Brooke knew she wasn't going back to the blue room. Pulling the afghan around her shoulders, she crept through the closet and opened the tower-room door.

An unheated room, Aunt Olive had called it, and yet to Mary Brooke it felt warm. Winter sunlight flooded through the window and onto the golden floor. The curved walls seemed to embrace her. She closed the door behind her and felt the quiet safety of it—her very own room.

Mary Brooke staggered to the seat shelf, her legs suddenly trembling. She stubbed off her shoes, put her glasses on the desk, and curled up, snuggled into the afghan, on the soft green sun-warmed cushion.

It was lies, all lies, all . . .

Mary Brooke slept.

# CHAPTER 10

# HIDEAWAY

She woke to the sound of the doorbell. It chimed, peal after peal, muffled here in the tower room, but insistent. Cautiously Mary Brooke raised her head, noon's events still throbbing in it, as fuddled and troubled as her dreams. She got to her knees and, keeping to one side of the window so that she couldn't be seen, she peered down at the little stone porch.

Whoever was ringing the doorbell was standing too close to the house to be seen from above. But Mary Brooke didn't think it sounded like a grown-up. Grown-ups rang once and waited and then rang again, politely. This person was leaning on the button, it sounded like.

Just then the top of a golden head appeared below. Mary Brooke reached for her glasses and put them on. It was Shandy Kohler, hatless but bundled in his red-and-black coat. What was *he* doing here? Mary Brooke could tell by the sunlight, still streaming through the window, that she hadn't been asleep long, surely not long enough for school to let out.

She ducked out of sight. Shandy was backing toward the sidewalk, his head tilted, looking up. She thought she could hear him calling, but she couldn't make out the words. She peeked around the window frame again. Yes, his mittened hand was cupped to his mouth. Then she saw it drop, saw him turn and march around the house. In a minute, she could hear pounding at the back door.

Should she let him in? Mary Brooke pulled the afghan tighter around her shoulders. He had heard, she thought. He had heard what Natalie Quinn said. He would want to know about it. Is it true? he would want to know, and Mary Brooke didn't want to talk about it, didn't even want to think about it just yet. Not until I'm not so tired, she thought, pulling off her glasses and lying down again on the seat shelf.

In a little while the pounding stopped, and Mary Brooke closed her eyes.

The next time Mary Brooke woke, it was to the opening and slamming shut of doors and the sound of voices. She heard the floors creaking with footsteps.

"Mary Brooke! Mary Brooke!" It was Aunt Olive's voice, and joined with it, in chorus and counterpoint, deeper and calmer, was a man's voice—Mr. Henderson. "Mary Brooke! Mary Brooke!"

Mr. Henderson! What was *he* doing here?

Mary Brooke sat up, her heart pounding, her head still aching and thick.

It couldn't be anywhere near five o'clock, Aunt Olive's usual coming-home time, nor even three o'clock, the time school let out. How had they gotten away? Mary Brooke wondered. Had Shandy told them about the scene in the cafeteria? Had he told them she wouldn't answer the door?

"Mary Brooke! Mary Brooke!"

She could hear Aunt Olive's shoes tapping on the wooden floor of the front bedroom. Her voice sounded high, frantic. Was it anger Mary Brooke was hearing? Or fear? She heard the closet door open, and her heart stopped.

"Mary Brooke! Mary Brooke!"

"Any sign of her?" That was Mr. Henderson.

"No, nothing. You looked in the basement?"

"What about friends? Anyone she might have run to if she was upset?"

"Since she clearly *didn't* run to me?" Mary Brooke could hear the bitterness in Aunt Olive's tone.

"Livvie. You *know* I didn't mean *that.*"

"But it's true, Jim. It's true. I just haven't been able to . . ."

The closet door closed, muffling Aunt Olive's voice. Mary Brooke began to breathe again.

She sat clutching the afghan around her. I should go out now, she thought, before they get any madder. But she didn't move. The voices were retreating, out of the front bedroom, she imagined, and down the hall.

Why hadn't Aunt Olive come on through the closet to look in the tower room? Mary Brooke wondered. Didn't it occur to her that Mary Brooke might have found the door in the closet? Or had she forgotten it herself? ". . . had it blocked off," she had told Mary Brooke. Perhaps Aunt Olive didn't know about this door but only about the trapdoor that was, indeed, blocked off.

Suddenly Mary Brooke realized she was hearing voices

again, this time from the other side of the tower room, the side next to the blue room. She crept off the seat shelf and put her head close to the wall.

". . . without a coat?" Aunt Olive's voice was saying. "She can't have gone far!"

"I think, Livvie, we'd better call the police."

Mary Brooke caught her breath. The police!

"Yes, of course, you're right. She's not at school. She's not here. She's not at the Kohlers'. I don't know where else to look. Oh, Ji-im!"

A funny noise was coming through the wall, a kind of harsh, choked sound. Mary Brooke pulled her head away from the wall. She didn't like hearing it.

They were going to call the police, she thought. This was getting out of hand. Now Aunt Olive really *would* be mad when they found her. . . . *If* they found her . . .

But they *will* find me, Mary Brooke thought, trailing back to the seat shelf. Her feet were cold, and she pulled them up under her and tucked the afghan around them.

I wish I could just stay here forever, Mary Brooke thought, hidden like Colin in *The Secret Garden*. Except that his father and the servants knew about Colin and took care of him. It was just Mary Lennox who didn't know. They brought food to him and books and games and . . . I suppose he had a bathroom of his own, thought Mary Brooke, suddenly aware that she needed to use the toilet.

I *can't* stay here forever, Mary Brooke thought, even if Aunt Olive doesn't know about the door. The sooner I go out, the less trouble I'm likely to be in. Only I'm already in a whole bunch of trouble, she thought. A whole big bunch . . .

Mary Brooke continued to huddle on the seat shelf,

unmoving. If only her head would quit aching. If only she hadn't run away from school this noon. If only stupid Natalie Quinn hadn't said those things about Mother . . .

She was startled to hear a car starting up in the driveway. Mary Brooke reached for her glasses and looked out the window. She was in time to see Aunt Olive's gray Buick pull into the street and drive away.

I thought they were going to call the police, Mary Brooke thought. I thought they were worried about me. She listened hard. Had they both gone? The house was silent. No voices, no footsteps, no slamming doors.

Mary Brooke tiptoed to the tower-room door and opened it softly. She listened. She crept through the dark closet, past the plastic garment bags, and opened the closet door. She listened.

They were gone. They had gone off and left her, just as though they didn't care that they couldn't find her. Her cheeks were suddenly hot with anger. Well, she'd show them! She dropped the afghan to the floor and kicked it back into the closet. Just see if she *ever* came out now! They'd find her someday, maybe, when they were tearing down the house. Just a skeleton in a hidden room, like the little English princes she had read about once. It would be a mystery who she was and why she was there. "The door was unlocked," they'd say. "She could have come out at any time, but she didn't. She didn't because of that aunt of hers. That cruel, cruel aunt!"

The telephone rang twice after Aunt Olive and Mr. Henderson had gone—shrill, persistent ringings—but of course Mary Brooke didn't answer it. She was busy using the bathroom and gathering supplies. She needed warm clothes, her old sweater and pants and flannel pajamas, fetched from the bottom of the Goodwill bag in the basement. She was careful to replace the discards exactly as she had found them so that Aunt Olive wouldn't be able to tell she had taken anything. She needed food. Would Aunt Olive notice that the extra jar of peanut butter was missing? Or an apple or two from the refrigerator fruit bin? What about a handful of cookies? She put the food into a brown paper sack with a few paper napkins and an empty fruit jar full of water. What else?

There was still the problem of the bathroom. Mary Brooke wrinkled her forehead with concentration as she carried the clothes and food back up to the tower room. Then suddenly the answer was right before her eyes, had been there all the time, she thought—the little stand beneath a window of the front bedroom. A commode, Mother had called the one like it that they had seen one day in an antique-shop window.

"Look, Brooksie," her mother had cried in delight, "your grandma had one just like it. It's what they had in the old days instead of a bathroom. The pitcher was for carrying water to the bowl, where you washed. And inside, in the cupboard beneath, there should be a chamber pot."

"A chamber pot?" Mary Brooke had said.

"Yes, love, can you imagine? Instead of a toilet they used the pot if they had to go in the night, and then emptied it in the morning." Her nose wrinkled, and her laugh rang out. "Aren't you glad we live in modern times?" she had cried, but Mary Brooke had not been so sure. She hated having to creep all the way down the long dark hall in the night to the bathroom they shared with Mrs. Scherer's other boarders. She worried that the flushing would disturb people. "Don't you think a thing about that," Mother had said. "We pay our rent the same as anyone else!" Except they didn't always. Not on time. Mary Brooke had lived in terror that Mrs. Scherer would say they'd have to move.

Now, her heart beating with hope, Mary Brooke set the food and clothes inside the closet with the heap of afghan. She went to the commode and opened its cupboard. There it was, what she was hoping for, a wide-rimmed china pot with pink flowers painted on its lid to match the pitcher and bowl on the marble top of the commode. She reached for it with trembling hands. Chances were Aunt Olive would never think to look for it. She never came into the front bedroom anyway. With this and food and clothes to keep her warm, Mary Brooke could stay in the tower room forever—or at least until Father comes, she thought. She'd have all day when Aunt Olive was at school to roam the house, but when Aunt Olive was at home she'd be safe in the tower room.

She had been so intent on her discovery that she didn't hear the car, but the slamming of the back door made her jump. What had gotten into Aunt Olive? She never let doors slam and had a fit when Mary Brooke did.

Mary Brooke scurried into the closet with the chamber pot, pulling the door carefully shut behind her. Then, silently, alert to the places where the floor squeaked, she carried her supplies into the tower room and crawled back onto the seat shelf, wrapped in the afghan, to listen and wait.

Aunt Olive called again. "Mary Brooke! Mary Brooke!" Mary Brooke imagined her standing at the foot of the stairs, her face tilted upward expectantly, as she did when she called Mary Brooke to supper. But she did not come upstairs again, and Mr. Henderson didn't call. Had he come back with her? Mary Brooke wondered. She heard voices, one deeper than the other. That must be him. Mary Brooke wondered again why he was there. She wondered what must be happening at school with two teachers suddenly absent. She wondered what the kids were saying. How long would they look for her? How soon before they forgot?

It was hard just sitting with nothing to do. Mary Brooke took down one or two of her books from the shelf above the desk and leafed through them, but she had read them so many times before. She wished she had her library book, abandoned on her lunch tray, she remembered. She wished they'd go away again so that she could move about freely, putting her things away and straightening up a bit. Mary Brooke hated mess, and the tower room was a mess right now, with the things she had brought jumbled beside the door and the books she had dumped out of one of the cardboard boxes yesterday for Perky still scattered on the floor.

The books . . . Mary Brooke cocked her head and looked more closely at the books. They were not the same books she had looked at that first time, the ones she had used for standing on when she cleaned. These were bigger, but not so thick, bound in leather, with heavy black pages. Not books, but albums. Photograph albums, she saw.

Just then the doorbell rang. She heard Aunt Olive's tapping footsteps almost running in the hall and the door opening. On her knees, once again Mary Brooke was looking down at the porch and once again saw no one. A murmur of voices, the door closing, and Shandy came walking off the porch. Mary Brooke measured the light with her eyes. School must be out now, she thought as a black-and-white police car pulled up to the curb.

Once again Mary Brooke's chest felt tight with her beating heart. They *had* called the police after all! Would the policemen search the house now and find her? She ducked down on the seat and crouched there, listening to the doorbell, the footsteps, the rumblings of voices below. It seemed hours before the policemen left, without searching the house, and hours more before she heard Mr. Henderson leave. In the meantime the phone kept ringing and ringing. There had not been so much excitement in this house since she had come to live here, Mary Brooke thought, feeling a little sorry that she was missing it.

Her muscles felt tight and twitchy. She longed to get up and walk around a little, even run. The light grew dimmer and dimmer. Soon she would not even be able to read, if she had something good to read, she thought. And then she remembered the albums.

Holding her breath, Mary Brooke leaned over the side of the seat shelf and reached for the nearest album, one that had slipped off the heap of albums and come to rest not far from where she sat. She was able to get hold of its edge and slide it toward her. It made a slithering sound against the floor, and Mary Brooke stopped and listened but heard nothing from downstairs. She pulled the album up onto her lap and held it there, feeling triumphant. It was something to do at least—looking at old pictures. Perhaps there would be pictures of Mother and Aunt Olive as little girls, or perhaps even a picture of her father! Eagerly Mary Brooke began to turn the pages.

The first pictures were of people Mary Brooke didn't know—an old man with frowning eyebrows and white whiskers and a round, serious-looking baby in high-topped shoes and some young girls with piled-up hair and old-fashioned dresses. Mary Brooke turned the pages, reading with interest the names and dates written in white ink under the photos—John Turnbull Brooke, 1849; and Thaddeus Benjamin Brooke, 1881; and Goldie Campbell and Edda Rollins, 1902. Thaddeus Benjamin. The name seemed familiar to Mary Brooke. It kept ringing in her mind, and she turned back to the baby. Of course! Judge Thaddeus B. Brooke! That was her grandfather. This plump, clear-eyed baby with a swirl of pale hair was her grandfather. Mary Brooke squinted at the photograph of the baby in the growing dusk. How strange to think that this little baby had grown up to be a judge and had married her grandmother and had two little girls—one of them Mary Brooke's mother and the other Aunt Olive—and had built this castle house and collected a cabinet full of little porcelain dishes and then had died. Once upon a time her dead grandfather had been a little baby. He had been ten years old like Mary Brooke. He had been a young man. . . .

Mary Brooke turned the pages forward, looking for the young man her grandfather had been, but it was dark now, too dark to see, and at last she laid down the album and realized she was hungry.

The telephone still rang from time to time, and when Aunt Olive answered it the next time, Mary Brooke crept to the paper sack by the door and, squatting on the floor beside it, ate an apple, some peanut butter she scooped from the jar with her finger, and two cookies. She drank some water from the bottle, wondering how long a person could live on peanut butter and fruit and cookies without getting some sort of vitamin deficiency—Miss Osgood had often warned them of the importance of good nutrition. Then she crept back to the seat shelf and wrapped herself once again in the afghan and lay down.

But this time she didn't fall straight to sleep. Beneath her she could hear Aunt Olive's pacing footsteps. I suppose she *is* worried, Mary Brooke thought, feeling half hopeful and half guilty that this was the case. Mary Brooke hardened her thoughts. It serves her right, she thought. It serves her right for being so . . . But she couldn't think just what it was about Aunt Olive that made her deserving of worry except that—it was a dumb thought, and Mary Brooke stifled it right away—except that she wasn't Mother.

# CHAPTER 11

# LIKE LOOKING INTO A MIRROR

The phone rang in the night, again and again. Mary Brooke could hear Aunt Olive's running footsteps each time she answered it. At least once the doorbell chimed. But in between times, Mary Brooke supposed, she slept. Once, she remembered, she opened her eyes to see snowflakes, huge and ghostly, drifting past the window. She felt cramped, her muscles tensed against falling off the seat shelf. She was cold. Sometime in the night she crept to the pile of old clothes and pulled the pants on under her dress and the pajama top over it before she again wrapped herself in the afghan and lay down. But her feet stayed icy all night, and her dreams disturbed her. Later she couldn't remember what she'd dreamed, but she knew she'd felt angry and scared and sad.

At last when she opened her eyes the tower room was gray with dawn, and the house was silent. She could feel the cold wall against her back. She had to go to the toilet.

The floor was cold too. She felt it through her socks as she squatted over the chamber pot. Her bottom cringed from the pot's icy rim, but she was glad she had thought to bring it into the tower room. What she had not thought of was toilet paper. She found a used tissue in her pocket. When Aunt Olive went off to school this morning, she thought, she'd have to get some more.

And then she remembered. If yesterday was Friday—and the tuna surprise left no doubt of that—then Aunt Olive wouldn't be going to school today. Nor tomorrow.

Mary Brooke looked bleakly at her remaining apple and cookies. Soon they would be gone. How long could a person live on just peanut butter? she wondered.

She sighed and stood up, stretching. Aunt Olive must be asleep, the house was so quiet. Mary Brooke would have to use this opportunity to move about. Otherwise, she thought, I'll stiffen into a board.

Her teeth were chattering, but she made herself drop the afghan she still clutched around her shoulders. I'll straighten things up a little, she thought as she picked up the afghan and folded it neatly to put on the seat shelf. She arranged her food on a bookshelf. She put the lid on the chamber pot and hid it—her nose wrinkled as she carried it—behind a box of books.

The photograph albums were too tall to fit on a bookshelf standing up, but Mary Brooke decided to stack them on a bottom shelf. As she moved them, two or three at a time, one album fell open, and as she closed it she caught a glimpse of a large family portrait.

She opened the album again and paged through it, looking for the portrait. There were some blurry, brownish snapshots of the castle, looking a little naked with no bushes or trees around it. In one, two little girls stood in the yard, holding hands.

In another, some children were gathered around a birthday cake on a table. That one had names and a date underneath it, written in white ink on the black page: Audrey, Tom, Bel, Betty Gilbert, Elsie, Jim, and Livvie, 9/26. Mary Brooke tried to make out which ones might be her mother and Aunt Olive, but the faces in the picture were small and dappled with sunlight and shadow.

Here were some pictures of children on a lakeshore in funny old-fashioned swimsuits. And then, turning the page, Mary Brooke found the photograph she was looking for—a man standing behind a seated woman in a dark dress who was looking at a book, and on either side of the woman, a little girl. Mary Brooke knew instantly which one was Mother and which Aunt Olive. Mother wasn't really looking at the book, she could tell, but was flirting from beneath her long lashes, a mischievous smile on her lips. Aunt Olive . . .

It was like looking into a mirror, Mary Brooke thought. Aunt Olive had had the same straight, colorless hair, the same narrow face, the same serious eyes and mouth as Mary Brooke. Mary Brooke examined the face of the little girl Aunt Olive had been. Sad, Mary Brooke thought. She looks sad. Do *I* look sad?

Thoughtfully she closed the album. She carried the last of the albums to the shelf, putting the one with the portrait on top.

The tower room was beginning to look the way she wanted it to be—tidy, she thought with satisfaction.

If only she could tidy herself! Aunt Olive would have noticed if her comb and brush were missing, or her new yellow toothbrush. She contented herself with combing back her hair with her fingers—she could feel its snarliness, but at least it was out of her eyes. She drank a little of the stale-tasting water from the jar, swishing it around in her mouth before she swallowed it. She wondered if she dared use some to wash her face, but she didn't have a washcloth either, and all the dust-rag underwear was full of dust. Finally she allowed herself to wrap back up in the afghan. Her shoes were still wet.

Little by little the room had grown light. Mary Brooke got onto her knees on the seat shelf, put on her glasses, and looked out the window. Once again the street lay under a thick carpet of snow. More cold, she thought, shivering, and could feel it through the window, which was frosted around its edges with a tracery of white.

Aunt Olive would be getting up soon, she thought. Or maybe not. Maybe she would sleep in. Certainly the phone had kept ringing late into the night. Perhaps Aunt Olive would be so tired she would sleep deeply and late. If she did, Mary Brooke thought, I could sneak down for some more food or . . .

Mary Brooke went to the little door. She knelt beside it and listened, but she could hear nothing. Then she remembered how she had heard Aunt Olive and Mr. Henderson yesterday through the wall. She scooted around to a space between bookshelves and put her ear to the wall. She listened and scooted and listened and scooted and listened until she was at the place where she had heard them yesterday, the wall nearest the blue room. Aunt Olive wouldn't be in the blue room, Mary Brooke thought, but still she put her ear to the wall and listened. And then drew back, startled.

She had heard something. Cautiously she laid her head

against the wall again. It was that sound, that ugly, choked sound.

This time Mary Brooke let herself know what she was hearing. It was crying. Aunt Olive *was* in the blue room, and she was crying.

Mary Brooke leaned back and stared at the wall. She swallowed hard, trying to push down the sick feeling that rose in her stomach.

So Aunt Olive did care, after all, that she couldn't find Mary Brooke. She cared enough to be crying, all alone. Mary Brooke hugged herself and rocked a little on her heels. She knew what that felt like, she thought—being all alone and worried when someone was late getting home, or maybe didn't come home at all. She had cried too, sometimes, waking to find Mother's place in the bed still cold and empty and the light beginning to come through the window.

Mary Brooke's stomach felt hollow and shaky. Her hands were shaky too, and her legs trembled when she stood up. She shuffled to the little door, and her hand slipped on the knob, turning it, but she knew that she had to go out. Aunt Olive needed her.

Aunt Olive was huddled on the white-and-gilt bed, her plain wool bathrobe looking oddly out of place against the blue satin spread. Her thin shoulders shuddered with her sobs.

Mary Brooke wanted to go to her and put her arms around her, but it took all her courage just to open her mouth and make the words come out. "Aunt Olive . . ."

Aunt Olive's whole body stilled. For a heartbeat she didn't move. Then, slowly, her head came up, and her face turned toward Mary Brooke. There was a blank look in her swollen eyes. Her face looked old and gray.

"Oh, Aunt Olive," Mary Brooke said. "I'm sorry."

There was a kind of strangling sound, and then, before Mary Brooke had time to blink, Aunt Olive was off the bed and folding her into her arms. "Mary Brooke, Mary Brooke!"

She's not mad, Mary Brooke thought in wonder. Aunt Olive's arms were around her, holding her tight. They rocked together, and Mary Brooke felt the wetness of their faces pressed together.

"I'm so sorry. . . ."

"Oh, Mary Brooke . . ."

". . . didn't mean . . ."

". . . back, you're back . . ."

". . . got scared . . ."

". . . thought I'd lost *you* too."

Aunt Olive's hands were moving over Mary Brooke's face, touching it as though Aunt Olive couldn't see enough of her with eyes alone. She felt Mary Brooke's arms and shoulders.

"Are you all right?" she was saying. "Truly all right? Where have you *been*?"

"Yes, yes, I'm fine," Mary Brooke said, and then she couldn't look at Aunt Olive's face as she told her, "I've been *here* all the time . . . in the tower room."

There was a silence, but Aunt Olive's arms stayed close and warm around her. "Here?" she said. "Here in the tower room?"

Mary Brooke nodded, her head against Aunt Olive's chest.

"The tower room?" Aunt Olive said. "But how . . ."

Finally Aunt Olive's arms were loosening. She stepped

back and looked at Mary Brooke and shook her head a little, as though trying to clear her thoughts. Mary Brooke thought she knew how Aunt Olive was feeling, as though too much was happening too quickly to keep it all quite straight.

Then, "You're cold," said Aunt Olive. "So am I."

Mary Brooke nodded. "I'll go turn up the heat," she said.

"And I'll make us some cocoa," said Aunt Olive. "Are you hungry, Mary Brooke?"

"A little," Mary Brooke admitted, her stomach rumbling.

Aunt Olive nodded briskly. "Yes," she said. "Breakfast. That's what we need. And then we'll sort this out."


They sat at the kitchen table, the warm cocoa mugs still cradled in their hands. Aunt Olive had turned on the oven and left its door open so that the kitchen was— toasty, Mary Brooke thought. She felt as though something frozen at her center had thawed.

"Another door to the tower room . . . ," Aunt Olive was saying, her voice bewildered. "I can't imagine why I've never discovered it, except that I haven't liked to go into the front bedroom since Mother died. It seemed a . . . a reproach to me. As though her wasting away as she did, grieving . . . as though it were my fault. . . ." She blinked and looked at Mary Brooke again, her eyes focusing. "Now that you tell me," she said, "I do remember. It was small. Even as a child I would have had to stoop to go through it. I think I must have thought it was a cupboard, not a door. We always used the little wrought-iron spiral stair and the trapdoor. . . ."

"Stair?" Mary Brooke said.

"Mother, your grandmother, had it removed," Aunt Olive said. "She had the opening in the living-room ceiling plastered over. . . ."

"But why?" said Mary Brooke.

Aunt Olive gazed into her cocoa mug. She swirled the dregs of chocolate and drained the mug and set it down.

Then she looked into Mary Brooke's eyes. The look was steady and sad, and it occurred to Mary Brooke that really, Aunt Olive had very nice eyes—clear and deep, where Mother's had been . . . shallow, Mary Brooke thought. You looked into Mother's eyes and what you saw was how Mother was feeling at that moment, nothing more.

"Mary Brooke," Aunt Olive said. "I think it is time we shared our ghosts."

"Ghosts?" said Mary Brooke.

Aunt Olive nodded. "I'm haunted, Mary Brooke, haunted by the past. I realized it last night, when I thought you had gone. When I thought you had run away from me, were lost and hurt or frozen or . . . or dead somewhere, and I couldn't help you. I realized suddenly that I was lost too . . . lost in the past with my ghosts."

Mary Brooke nodded. Yes, she thought she knew what Aunt Olive was saying. Ghosts were like Mother, who still felt so alive to Mary Brooke, even though she was dead.

Dead.

Mary Brooke felt it for the first time, with a startling pain that took her breath away. Mother was dead. Like Perky. Her body was cold and still, and her—spirit, Mary Brooke thought, remembering Shandy's words—her spirit had gone away. She was never coming back. Never.

Didn't I know that before? Mary Brooke wondered when she had caught her breath.

The telephone was ringing. Aunt Olive pushed back her chair and went to answer it. Mary Brooke got up from the table and began to carry their things to the sink.

"Yes," Aunt Olive's voice was saying from the hall. "Yes, Jim, she's been here all along. . . . Yes, I'll explain later. I called the police and told them. No . . . No, not right now. I think we need a little time, just Mary Brooke and I. . . . Of course. Yes. That would be fine. And . . . and, thank you, Jim . . . for . . . for everything. Good-bye."

Mary Brooke was rinsing the dishes when Aunt Olive came back into the kitchen.

"That was Mr. Henderson," she said. "He's been worried."

Mary Brooke nodded. She didn't look at Aunt Olive. She really had been a great deal of trouble, she thought. Mr. Henderson. The police.

"Would you like to get freshened up a little?" Aunt Olive said.

Did this mean that Aunt Olive wasn't going to "share her ghosts" after all? She seemed brisk now, distant, as though the telephone had brought her back to her old self.

"I don't care," said Mary Brooke.

"Tell you what," said Aunt Olive. "Let's run you a bath, and while you get cleaned up, I'll dress. Okay?"

"I don't care," said Mary Brooke.

# CHAPTER 12
# GHOSTS

The hot bath made Mary Brooke feel warm and limp. Aunt Olive, wearing a sweater and slacks, helped her to towel dry. She had brought pants and a warm shirt into the bathroom for Mary Brooke.

"Are these all right?" she said, and Mary Brooke couldn't help thinking that Mother wouldn't have asked. She'd just have brought what she wanted Mary Brooke to wear and told her to put them on.

When she was dressed Mary Brooke picked up her brush and began to pull at the snarls in her hair, not looking into the mirror. Suddenly she felt Aunt Olive's hand, warm over hers.

"May I help you?" Aunt Olive said.

Mary Brooke looked into the mirror and saw Aunt Olive standing behind her. "I look like you," Mary Brooke said.

Aunt Olive nodded and began to stroke the brush

through Mary Brooke's hair. "Yes," she said. "I think you do a little."

The brush worked gently at the snarls. Aunt Olive didn't yank with impatience as Mother would have done.

"My mother was beautiful," said Mary Brooke.

"Yes," said Aunt Olive. "Yes, she was."

Mary Brooke watched her hair silken under the brush. It made tiny crackling sounds and followed the brush like something alive. Aunt Olive put down the brush and smoothed Mary Brooke's hair with her hands.

"It's long enough to braid," she said. "Would you like me to braid it for you, Mary Brooke?"

Mary Brooke nodded. She didn't want Aunt Olive to stop.

Aunt Olive picked up the comb and drew it down the back of Mary Brooke's head, from her crown to her nape in a long, straight line that felt sharp and neat to Mary Brooke. She closed her eyes.

"When I was a little girl," Aunt Olive said, "I thought your mother was the most beautiful girl in the world."

There was a silence as Aunt Olive's fingers worked in Mary Brooke's hair, dividing, tugging, twining the strands smoothly into a braid. Mary Brooke kept her eyes closed.

"Everyone else thought so too," said Aunt Olive. "My mother. My father. We all adored her. We spoiled her. Especially my father. He couldn't say no to her. . . ."

Mary Brooke opened her eyes and looked into the mirror. Behind her, Aunt Olive's face had twisted. She was looking at the strands of hair she held in her hands.

"I was jealous," she said softly. "I thought he loved her more than me. I had been first, you know, the only child for a while, and then she came along, and he seemed to . . . you know, he seemed to forget about me. At least, I thought so."

"Mother was always the center of attention," Mary Brooke said. "People never noticed me."

Aunt Olive looked into the mirror and met Mary Brooke's eyes. She nodded.

"I tried very hard to please him," she told Mary Brooke. "I would have done anything . . . but she had all the advantages—her looks, her voice, her . . . gaiety? Was that what it was? And they were alike, Father and Isabel— vivacious and impractical. If it hadn't been for Mother, I doubt Father would have stayed with the law. He was a dreamer. . . . I was like Mother, the sensible one."

Like me, Mary Brooke thought.

"And yet I loved her," Aunt Olive said, her voice breaking. "How could one help but love her?"

Mary Brooke felt a tear tickle down her cheek. Aunt Olive was putting a rubber band around the end of the braid. Then she turned Mary Brooke in her arms and hugged her. "You too," she said. "You loved her very much."

And Mary Brooke was crying hard. Crying and crying. But this time the tears felt warm and soft and . . . cleansing, Mary Brooke thought later. They seemed to wash the bitterness away.

Mary Brooke had had a nap. It seemed a funny time for a nap, right in the middle of a Saturday morning, but she was so tired.

"I could use a little rest myself," Aunt Olive had said, and they had lain down together on Aunt Olive's narrow brown bed.

When Mary Brooke woke she was alone.

For a moment she felt frightened, and then she heard Aunt Olive downstairs, rattling things in the kitchen.

Mary Brooke got up and went into the bathroom to see if her braids were still neat. A little bit of hair had pulled loose around her face, but it looked kind of nice, Mary Brooke thought. Kind of soft and pretty. She tucked in her shirt and went downstairs to find Aunt Olive.

"Mr. Henderson is coming for lunch," Aunt Olive said. "He wants to see for himself that you are all right. He was tremendously worried."

"Why?" said Mary Brooke.

Aunt Olive turned away from the stove, where she had been stirring some soup. She looked into Mary Brooke's eyes with her clear, straight look.

"Because he cares about you, Mary Brooke. Don't you know that?"

Mary Brooke didn't answer. She went to the silverware drawer and pulled it open.

"Should I set the table in the dining room?" she said.

*Cares about you. Cares about you.* The words sang in Mary Brooke's head as she went back and forth from the kitchen to the dining room. She could feel a little smile inside of her, though she was careful to keep it off her face.

"You were going to tell me why Grandmother blocked off the tower room," she said to Aunt Olive as she got the butter dish out of the refrigerator.

Aunt Olive was stirring the soup again. The spoon went round and round, and for a moment she didn't answer.

"Yes," she said. "Yes, I was." She didn't turn to look at Mary Brooke, but her voice went on smoothly. "It's because that's where my father fell, on the stairs to the tower room. We'd just gotten the telegram, you see. The one from your mother, saying she had gone to Chicago, and I had taken it up to him—he was working at his little desk in the tower room—and he read it and came tearing down, distraught, and his heel caught"—Aunt Olive's voice was rushing on, as though to get the words out quickly before they could hurt her anymore—"caught on the stair, and he fell, and his neck . . ." Suddenly her voice broke, and she stopped. Then, slowly, she turned her head, and Mary Brooke saw a kind of wondering look in her eyes.

"Why . . . why, I've just realized," she said. "I've been blaming myself, as well as Isabel, for that. I've thought, all these years, if only I hadn't taken the telegram up. . . . I knew it was from Bel. I knew she was in trouble, and I thought, *now* he'll realize that *I'm* the good daughter. *Now* . . . now he'll love *me* best. . . ." She laughed softly, but Mary Brooke thought it wasn't a happy laugh. "What self-importance," Aunt Olive said. "To be thinking of myself, looking for the advantage for me in *her* misfortune . . . I've been blaming myself all this time. . . ."

It seemed to Mary Brooke that Aunt Olive was talking more to herself than to Mary Brooke. She stood at the stove, stirring the soup, half turned toward Mary Brooke, but her eyes were fixed on a time long ago.

"I suppose that's why I haven't changed the house," she was saying softly, wonderingly. "Did I think I didn't deserve a home? Did I think I was to blame for every-thing? His death, Mother's grief, Bel's leaving us?" Suddenly she was looking at Mary Brooke again. "I wasn't to blame, was I? No more than you are to blame for . . . for anything. No more than your mother was to blame for not being able to find your father. It was wartime, and we were all caught up in it, and she was so young, so full of life and hope. . . . What else could she do but go away and pretend she was married and live . . . as best she could?"

Mary Brooke put the butter dish down on the counter so that she wouldn't drop it.

"*Pretend* she was married?" she said.

Aunt Olive looked straight into her eyes. Mary Brooke could see the sympathy in her face.

"Yes," she said gently. "Didn't you know, Mary Brooke?"

"But what about our name?" Mary Brooke said. "Edwards. That's my father's name—Mr. Edwards."

Aunt Olive came to Mary Brooke and took her hands.

"Edward," she said. "Ed, actually. That's all she knew—just a soldier named Ed, passing through Kirkland one night on his way to his next posting."

Mary Brooke's knees felt weak.

"But . . . but someday he's going to come for me," she said.

Aunt Olive shook her head sadly. "No, Mary Brooke. He doesn't even know you exist. I'm so sorry. I assumed you knew."

Mary Brooke was shaking her head too. Trying to get hold of it. Somewhere there was a man who was her father, but he didn't even know he had a daughter. So he couldn't rescue her, nor could he ever have come back to live with them, as she used to dream in Chicago.

"Did Isabel tell you your father was going to come for you?" Aunt Olive said.

"No."

No, she never talked about him, Mary Brooke had to admit. I made it up, she thought. I made it up because I wanted him to come.

Aunt Olive was hugging her. "Poor Mary Brooke," she said. "How much should one little girl have to bear? I'm so sorry, sweetheart. I'd do anything to fix it for you if I could. I think your mother would have fixed it too, if it had been in her power."

Yes, Mary Brooke thought. That was what she was trying to do with "Uncle" Steve and all the others. Fix it for me . . . and for her. "We'll be so happy," she used to say. . . .

". . . She just did what she always did about the things in life she didn't like," Aunt Olive was saying. "She pretended it wasn't so. She pretended you had a father and that they'd been married and . . ."

The doorbell chimed.

Mary Brooke pulled away from Aunt Olive.

"May I go upstairs a minute?" she said. "Just a minute?"

"Of course," said Aunt Olive.


Mary Brooke was drawn to the tower room as though by a magnet. She needed it. It was her princess tower, her own magic place where rescue would come. . . .

But when she opened the door its smell assailed her—stale and disenchanted.

The chamber pot, she remembered, and hurried to carry it out, to empty it into the toilet, to rinse it and put it away in the commode where she had found it.

She crawled back through the closet. But still she did

not like the smell of the tower room. She climbed onto the seat shelf and worked at the window latch until she had loosened it and could swing the window open a bit. The clean, cold air rushed in, and Mary Brooke welcomed it. It cleared her head, she thought, huddling herself on the seat.

Downstairs she could hear Aunt Olive's and Mr. Henderson's voices. They were talking about her, she imagined. Pitying her.

Well, they needn't! She was just fine. She was! Here in her princess tower, she was safe from . . . she was safe . . . she was . . .

It didn't work. Even in the tower room Mary Brooke knew the truth. Mother was really, truly dead. And she had no father. No one to rescue her.

She put her face in her hands, but she wasn't crying. She was thinking a startling thought.

Rescue me from what? she thought.

From the castle?

I like the castle, Mary Brooke thought. I know it's not really a castle, but I like it anyway.

From Aunt Olive?

What was so bad about Aunt Olive? I think she might love me, Mary Brooke thought. I think . . . I *think* I might love her.

From room 13?

Suddenly, Mary Brooke knew she had gotten used to room 13 and to Mr. Henderson, who—cares about me, Mary Brooke thought.

Mary Brooke took her hands from her face and looked around her.

I'm just as bad as Mother, she thought. What had Aunt

Olive said? "She did what she always did about the things she didn't like. She pretended. . . ."

I've been pretending, Mary Brooke thought.


There was one more thing. As Mary Brooke went down the stairs toward the grown-ups' voices, she knew she'd have to find out.

# CHAPTER 13

# MISCHIEF

"You had us pretty worried, young lady," said Mr. Henderson in that pretend-angry voice of his. "After lunch I've got to see this hidey-hole of yours."

"*After* lunch," said Aunt Olive firmly, carrying in the bowls of soup. "I want to see this door I didn't even know was in my own house. . . ." Her voice faded, and then, thoughtfully, she said, "It *is* my own house, isn't it? Not Father's." She seemed to shake herself. "But first I've *got* to eat. I don't know about you two, but I'm absolutely starved!"

Suddenly Mary Brooke realized she was starved too. The rich tomatoey soup; the beautiful crisp slices of red-and-white apple; the hot, chewy bread seemed the most scrumptious meal she had ever eaten. She spooned the soup into her mouth and felt it travel, warm and satisfying, to her middle.

As she looked across the table at Aunt Olive and Mr.

Henderson, none of them, it seemed, could stop smiling. Once again, so that Mr. Henderson could hear it, she had to tell how she had found the tower-room door. "I shouldn't have told all those lies, Aunt Olive. I'm sorry," said Mary Brooke.

And Mr. Henderson had to tell how Shandy Kohler had told him that Mary Brooke had gone from school without her coat, and how he had excused Shandy from class and sent him after her, only Shandy said she hadn't gone home, so he had had to tell Aunt Olive, and how Aunt Olive had been so upset that he was afraid to let her drive home alone, and so Mrs. Brunskill had taken over Aunt Olive's class and Mrs. Field had taken his, and they, he and Aunt Olive, had both gone looking for her.

"But you left again," Mary Brooke said. "You came home, but then you left, and I thought you didn't care after all."

Aunt Olive looked reproachful. "Mary Brooke, how *could* you think that?"

"It occurred to me you might have run to the park," Mr. Henderson said. "We went searching but came right back and called the police when we couldn't find you."

"I'm sorry," said Mary Brooke. "I'm sorry I caused so much trouble."

"I'm not," said Aunt Olive, pushing back her chair. She laid her napkin on the table. "You woke me up, Mary Brooke. I was acting like a fool. You made me realize how much I love you and how empty my life was before you came and how glad I am now that you're"—she hesitated a moment, looking carefully at Mary Brooke as though trying to decide whether or not to say it—"that you're *mine*," she said at last, and Mary Brooke felt so dizzy with gladness that she could only look back, hoping that how she felt was in her eyes.

They were halfway up the stairs when the telephone rang.

"Go on," Aunt Olive said. "I'll be up in a minute."

It was funny to see how Mr. Henderson had to fold himself almost double to get through the little door.

"Jumping Jehoshaphat!" he said. "If I get stuck, you'll have to pull and your aunt can push to get me out, the way they rescued Winnie-the-Pooh when he got stuck in Rabbit's hole."

Mary Brooke laughed. She didn't know that story, but it sounded funny.

Mr. Henderson stretched, his hand on the small of his back.

"I see why *that* door wasn't used much," he said.

Then he looked around.

"Well, well, well," he said. "This is a tower for a princess!"

Mary Brooke was startled.

"That—that's what *I* pretended," she said. "This was my princess tower, and the house was a castle with a dungeon and a secret passage and . . . But I'm not going to pretend anymore."

Mr. Henderson sat down on the seat shelf and held out his hand to her. She took it and came close.

"Mary Brooke," he said, "there is absolutely nothing wrong with pretending, so long as you *know* that's what you're doing. Pretending can be wonderful fun, and there's nothing wrong with fun."

"But . . . ," said Mary Brooke. "But I think that sometimes I didn't know I was pretending. I think I fooled myself."

"Well, that's something else," Mr. Henderson said. "That's not facing the truth. You are smart enough and strong enough to do both, I think."

"My word!" said Aunt Olive, crouching through the door. "My word!" She sighed, and Mary Brooke thought the sigh must mean that Aunt Olive was glad to see the tower room again after so long. She had a sort of bemused look on her face. "It looks beautiful," she said. "You must have worked so hard."

"Do you suppose we could close the window, though?" Mr. Henderson said. "It's a great room for Eskimos as it is, of course, but I forgot to bring my parka!" He reached up and drew the window closed as Aunt Olive's laugh rang out.

She was looking all around. "Are those boxes of books?" she said. "Father's books?"

Mary Brooke nodded. "And photo albums," she said, pointing to the bottom shelf where they were stacked. "You looked just like me when you were a little girl, Aunt Olive."

Mr. Henderson was nodding. "She's right, Livvie. It's why I liked her the moment I saw her. She reminds me of the girl I fell in love with."

Aunt Olive looked at him and then smiled, sadly.

"You were in love with Isabel," she said.

Mary Brooke thought that they had forgotten *her* entirely, they were gazing so intently at one another.

"No," said Mr. Henderson, his voice firm. "Not Isabel."

Mary Brooke looked from Aunt Olive to Mr.

Henderson and back to Aunt Olive. Aunt Olive's hands were fluttering at her throat.

"Oh, Jim!" she said.

Then Mary Brooke saw that she had remembered her. "I . . . we . . ." Aunt Olive faltered and turned away from him.

"Mary Brooke!" Now her voice was brisk and unnaturally loud. Mary Brooke saw that her face was crimson. "You've certainly made this room your own, Mary Brooke," she said. "But you need a chair for your desk, it seems to me, and a great many more books. I always wondered what Mother had done with Father's books and the old photo albums and Isabel's and my books from when we were children. Are they here too? Did you look, Mary Brooke?"

Mary Brooke shook her head.

"Well, we will then," Aunt Olive said, still talking fast. "I think this could be your little study if we put in a heater. Perhaps you'd like to move into the front bedroom to sleep? We could change the curtains and the furniture. In fact, it wouldn't hurt to redecorate *my* room too. . . ."

She seemed to give herself a little shake, and Mary Brooke saw that still Aunt Olive was not looking at Mr. Henderson, though he continued to gaze at her. She was laughing ruefully.

"It might help me to banish some of those ghosts we were talking about, to make some changes," she said. "Mother and Father and Bel are gone, but *you* and *I* are here."

"And I am here, Livvie," Mr. Henderson said.

Now, finally, Aunt Olive was looking at him.

"Yes, Jim," she said, her voice low and—tender, Mary Brooke thought. "Yes, Jim, you are," she said.

But Aunt Olive's words were still ringing in Mary Brooke's mind. *To banish some of those ghosts,* she had said.

"Aunt Olive," Mary Brooke said, barely able to get the words out. "Aunt Olive, there's something else. . . ."

"Yes, sweetheart?"

Aunt Olive was sitting down on the seat shelf beside Mr. Henderson, and they were looking at each other, not at Mary Brooke.

Mary Brooke chewed her lip.

"Natalie Quinn said . . ." The words sounded bumpy, as though they had to come over the lump in her throat. "Natalie said Mother died . . . because she had an . . . abortion."

She heard the sharp intake of Aunt Olive's breath, and Mary Brooke's heart began to pound. She wished she could take the word back, but . . .

"Yes." Aunt Olive's voice was so quiet that Mary Brooke wasn't sure she had heard it.

"She said it was Mother's . . . punishment . . . because she killed her baby . . . that she died."

Mr. Henderson reached out and pulled Mary Brooke close to him and Aunt Olive.

"Mother wouldn't kill a baby!" Mary Brooke cried, burying her face against Mr. Henderson's shirt.

"Of course she wouldn't," Mr. Henderson said, rubbing her back with his big warm hand. "I don't think she thought about it that way at all. I think she was desperate and scared. . . ."

Mary Brooke remembered the frantic look in Mother's eyes those last days. It was all Mother was ever able to do just to take care of herself and me, she thought. In fact, a lot of the time *I* took care of *her.* How *could* we have managed with a little baby? Mary Brooke wondered, feeling suddenly torn between the idea of a sweet baby sister or brother and the knowledge that indeed they wouldn't have been able to keep and care for it. Yes, Mother *must* have been scared, Mary Brooke thought.

"I think she just didn't know what else to do," Mr. Henderson said.

"But then why was she punished?" Mary Brooke cried, pulling back from him so that she could see if the truth was in his eyes.

"She wasn't," Mr. Henderson said. "She died because in our country abortion is against the law. So she couldn't go to a proper doctor. It had *nothing* to do with punishment." Mr. Henderson's voice was fierce, and he was looking straight back at Mary Brooke. "Your mother needed help . . . and didn't find it. *That* is why she died."

Aunt Olive was crying. Mary Brooke, glancing at her, saw the tears spilling down her face.

"I could have helped her," Aunt Olive said in a whisper.

Mr. Henderson put an arm around Aunt Olive's shoulders. His other arm was still around Mary Brooke.

"We all make mistakes, Livvie," he said. "Isabel, me, even you."

Aunt Olive nodded her head.

"It's not too late to forgive her," Mr. Henderson said. "And yourself." He looked back at Mary Brooke. "You too, Mary Brooke," he said. "You could forgive them both."

Mary Brooke nestled with Aunt Olive in the circle of Mr. Henderson's arms.

Yes, she thought. I could.

\* \* \*

133

Mary Brooke sat curled in Grandfather's chair. Aunt Olive had said she might. "*That* ghost's banished for good," she had said.

Mr. Henderson was in the kitchen with Aunt Olive, helping to fix supper. Mary Brooke could hear them, and it was a happy, comfortable sound.

Open on her lap, Mary Brooke held a book, a copy of *Winnie-the-Pooh* that Aunt Olive had found in one of the tower-room boxes when she heard that Mary Brooke had never read it. There were lots of other books in the boxes—good books, Mary Brooke thought. I should have looked more carefully and not jumped to conclusions, she thought. She could hardly wait to begin reading them. But now she couldn't seem to concentrate on reading. She felt—what was it Aunt Olive had said? Wrung out? Yes, that was it—wrung out like a dishrag, limp and spent.

Then the doorbell chimed.

"Will you get that please, Mary Brooke?" Aunt Olive called.

Mary Brooke unfolded her legs and put the book, open, on the chair arm, careful out of habit not to muss the antimacassar. She went to the door.

It was Shandy Kohler, grinning from ear to ear. In his arms was a box, and from inside the box came scratching sounds and shrill little mews.

"You got a new cat!" Mary Brooke cried before Shandy could open his mouth.

Shandy nodded.

"Wait'll you see!" he said.

Shandy put the box down in the middle of the entry. He plopped onto the floor beside it and opened the box flaps. He lifted out a tiny kitten, splotched with orange and black and white, just as Perky had been.

"Oh!" cried Mary Brooke. "Oh, Shandy, it's so cute. Is it a boy or a girl?"

But Shandy didn't answer. He set the kitten on the floor and reached into the box again. This time he lifted out a pale buff kitten, its fur standing on end like dandelion fluff.

"Two!" cried Mary Brooke.

"This one's the boy," said Shandy, pointing to the buff kitten, who was wobbling away as fast as he could. "And this one's the girl." He picked up the calico kitten and held her against his chest.

The calico kitten was purring. Mary Brooke would not have thought something so little could make so loud a sound. "Some motor!" Mary Brooke said.

"Which one do you want?" said Shandy.

Mary Brooke looked at Shandy, certain she could not have heard him right.

"You can have one of them," Shandy said. "Which?"

"But," said Mary Brooke. "But, Aunt Olive . . ."

"Is this yours?" said Aunt Olive from the kitchen doorway. She was holding the buff kitten in her hands, and there was a big smile on her face. Behind her, Mr. Henderson grinned over her shoulder.

Mary Brooke jumped up and ran to get the kitten.

"When I talked to Mrs. Kohler on the telephone earlier this afternoon," Aunt Olive said, "she wanted to know if you might have a kitten. I told her you are a responsible child, and I thought you might . . . if you take care of it."

Mary Brooke reached for the kitten, and Aunt Olive put him into her outstretched hands.

"Truly?" Mary Brooke breathed.

"Truly," said Aunt Olive.

Mary Brooke turned the kitten around so that she

could look into his face. His tiny mouth opened in a yawn, showing sharp, white teeth. His pink tongue darted out, and he licked Mary Brooke's finger. It felt like a tickle.

"Oh!" said Mary Brooke.

"So which one do you want?" said Shandy. "Living next door to each other, they won't get lonesome. That was my idea, since Ma said I can only have one. I figure we can play with them together, maybe take them to school on Pet Day and . . ."

School.

It was going to be hard to go back to school and have to face Natalie and the other kids. Mary Brooke pushed away the thought of it. Mr. Henderson would be there, she reminded herself, and Shandy, and it would be fun to take her very own kitten to Pet Day. . . . Mary Brooke wondered if Natalie Quinn had a kitten. She rather hoped not.

"Which one?" said Shandy again.

Mary Brooke looked at the calico kitten, curled in Shandy's lap as though she belonged there, quiet and gentle-looking. The buff kitten wriggled in Mary Brooke's hands.

"He wants to get down and explore," said Mr. Henderson.

Mary Brooke put the kitten down onto the floor. Immediately he began to bat at her shoelaces with his tiny paws. He lost his balance and rolled over on his back, then righted himself with a little shake and a small, surprised "mew." Mary Brooke laughed out loud.

"That one's going to be mischief," Aunt Olive said.

Mary Brooke looked at her to see whether Aunt Olive meant that she didn't like the buff kitten, but Aunt Olive was smiling.

"A little mischief wouldn't hurt this household," she said.

"A little mischief wouldn't hurt Mary Brooke," said Mr. Henderson.

Mary Brooke picked up the buff kitten again. She held his softness against her cheek.

"This one, Shandy, if you don't mind," she said.

Shandy looked relieved. "I really like this one best," he admitted. "I already named her. Perky the Second. What do you think?"

Mary Brooke smiled. "This is Mischief," she said. "Mischief the First."